Other Books By Lexi Blake

ROMANTIC SUSPENSE

Masters And Mercenaries
The Dom Who Loved Me
The Men With The Golden Cuffs
A Dom is Forever
On Her Master's Secret Service
Sanctum: A Masters and Mercenaries Novella
Love and Let Die
Unconditional: A Masters and Mercenaries Novella
Dungeon Royale
Dungeon Games: A Masters and Mercenaries Novella
A View to a Thrill
Cherished: A Masters and Mercenaries Novella
You Only Love Twice
Luscious: Masters and Mercenaries~Topped
Adored: A Masters and Mercenaries Novella
Master No
Just One Taste: Masters and Mercenaries~Topped 2
From Sanctum with Love
Devoted: A Masters and Mercenaries Novella
Dominance Never Dies
Submission is Not Enough
Master Bits and Mercenary Bites~The Secret Recipes of Topped
Perfectly Paired: Masters and Mercenaries~Topped 3
For His Eyes Only
Arranged: A Masters and Mercenaries Novella
Love Another Day
At Your Service: Masters and Mercenaries~Topped 4
Master Bits and Mercenary Bites~Girls Night
Nobody Does It Better, Coming February 20, 2018
Close Cover, Coming April 10, 2018
Protected, Coming July 31, 2018

Lawless
Ruthless
Satisfaction
Revenge

Away From Me

Lexi Blake
writing as
Sophie Oak

Away From Me
Published by DLZ Entertainment LLC

Copyright 2018 DLZ Entertainment LLC
Edited by Chloe Vale
ISBN: 978-1-937608-77-4

This is a work of fiction. Names, places, characters and incidents are the product of the author's imagination and are fictitious. Any resemblance to actual persons, living or dead, events or establishments is solely coincidental.

RPB OAK

Dedication

For the survivors
For those still fighting
For those who lost – for my father who I still miss every single
day

Foreword

Away From Me was the odd man out the first time it was published. It wasn't set in the same universe as Texas Sirens or Bliss. It was a book that came to me in a dream I had in London of all places. And yes, I dreamed of the gazebo scene and Gaby's reason for leaving Cal. When I woke up, I started writing even as my husband was leaving for work. I was over there for a week, but I ended up writing much of this novella while watching the London streets from my hotel room. I remember it was cold that spring, but I could feel the warmth of the Caribbean. At its core, *Away From Me* is my hope that everyone deserves a happily ever after and that love, even when it's hard, heals all wounds. I eventually brought this little one off into my Texas Sirens world. Later, in *Siren Unleashed*, you'll get an update on how these two are doing, but I thought it would be fun to include them in Masters and Mercenaries as well, so look for a little cameo from one of the originals in this book. And who knows, perhaps later my spies will need to go to a small island in the Caribbean where the nights are kinky and everything seems possible…

Prologue

"Do you love me?"

The question stopped Callum Reed in his tracks. He'd been ready to lean down and fuse his mouth to hers, to complete the final portion of the act. He liked this part more than he cared to admit, this moment when the world seemed to still and everything narrowed to him and her.

But that one question chilled his warm bed and made everything they'd done before feel meaningless.

He stared down at the woman who'd recently screamed her climax in his arms and everything inside him tensed. She'd never asked the question before, never mentioned the "L" word unless she was talking about Italian food or her favorite rom com.

He was not ready for this.

"Go to sleep, Gabrielle," he ordered in his deepest voice. He was in control and this was not happening now.

He pulled her into his arms. Something was going on with her this evening. Perhaps it was the book she was reading. Romantic drivel. Maybe it was because her birthday was coming up and she was feeling sentimental. It didn't matter because this wasn't something he was going into with her. Not now. Not ever.

In the morning, things would be back to normal. He'd go to work and Gaby would do…whatever it was she did all day. The crisis would pass and they would go back to normal.

She was an obedient girl. It was the very reason he'd chosen her as his submissive. She nestled down in his arms, finding her place there. She fit against him like a puzzle piece finding its home, but her

11

breathing didn't calm. There was a tightness to her body that should have been eased by the sex of mere moments before. Cal tried soothing her. He smoothed her hair down and kissed her ear, enjoying how soft she felt against him.

She sat up suddenly. The gray-green eyes that stared down at him were so serious, he wished he'd turned the light off. "I'm not letting you put this off. I deserve an answer. Do you love me, Cal?"

He threw an arm over his eyes and sighed. Something had her riled up and it was obvious he wasn't going to have any peace until he fixed it. "What do you want?"

"I want the truth. I've lived with you for three years now." Gaby's voice was unsteady, lilting up and down, an unmistakable clue to her emotional state.

Please don't cry. She'd been crying a lot lately. He would come home and find the evidence, but when he asked her, she would simply give him a smile that didn't reach her eyes and tell him she was all right.

He didn't like it when she cried.

"Are you ever going to ask me to marry you?"

Of course, he also didn't like it when she attempted to change the boundaries of their relationship.

He sat up and started to look for his pants. Of all the things she could say, this was the one most likely to get him moving. "No. I was very clear about that. I have no intentions of ever marrying again."

"Because you loved your wife and you won't ever love another woman?"

A hard knot sat in his chest. He wasn't sure if that knot was about his wife, Cassie, or the fact that he was about to have a prolonged fight with Gabrielle. Gabrielle was a sweet girl and he enjoyed her, but he would never allow himself to love anyone again. He'd had his chance with a woman and she died. The thought of marrying Gabrielle, of being that close…he couldn't go through that again. He'd known he couldn't and that was why he'd structured his relationship with Gabrielle the way he had.

He wanted her, but he knew his limits. He needed his distance. "I was up-front and honest with you, Gabrielle. I never told you this was going past where it is now. You have a collar. It's the only piece of jewelry I ever intend to buy you."

There was a moment of silence and then she seemed to find more courage. "Do you ever want to have children with me?"

The knot in his chest threatened to burst and rip him apart.

He slapped at the nightstand, unable to stem the tide of emotion the question brought out in him. "I don't want children. I made that plain. We signed a contract. We spent hours discussing what we wanted out of this relationship and it wasn't only me doing the talking. I provide everything for you. I provide you with a home, a car, your clothes…"

"And I act as your wife," she returned with some fire of her own. She sat up in bed, getting to her knees. Normally it was a position that signaled her submission, but there was nothing submissive about her now. Her chin was up and she hid not an inch of her body from him, meeting him stare for stare. Her gorgeous breasts were flushed a pretty pink and he forced his eyes away from them. "Don't pretend like I lie around all day. I keep the house and host your parties. I make dinner every night. I keep your books."

He got out of bed and started to pace. He should have seen this coming. He should have known it was only a matter of time before she made her play, but then he'd fucking fooled himself into thinking she was different from other women. He'd stupidly congratulated himself on finding the one woman in the world who didn't need a ring on her finger and access to every dime of his wealth to be happy. She'd seemed to need him, to need who he was as a Dom.

She'd been exquisitely patient. Three years she'd waited to spring her trap.

"So now you want a ring in exchange for domestic servitude." He shoved down all the feelings she'd brought out when she'd mentioned children, allowing the heartache to morph into something he could handle. Bitterness. Anger. Yes, he was well acquainted with those. "Well, sweetheart, next time don't sell yourself so cheaply. There's an old saying here in Texas about paying for milk…"

"Don't." Her shoulders fell and all the fire she'd shown seemed to disappear, her voice going quiet. "Don't compare me to a cow. I just wanted to know, okay?"

The moment lengthened, the silence so full of emotion he

couldn't stand it. They didn't need to do this. She didn't need that dull look in her eyes when everything was quite good between them.
She'd made her play. He'd explained it wouldn't work, but he found he couldn't shut her down entirely. He dropped to one knee in front of her, letting his hands drift to her legs. The contact comforted him as it had every day for the last three years.

She was still here. He could keep her. "Let's start this over again. Baby, just because I don't want to get married again doesn't mean I don't care about you."

A little spark animated her face. "You do?"

"Of course." He had to deal with her gently. Perhaps he hadn't praised her enough, told her how content he was with her.

There was a way out of this mess that question had made. He simply had to find the right thing to say to get her back to normal.

Because he was quite surprised at how desperately he wanted normal.

He would have told anyone who asked that if his sub gave him trouble, he would simply dismiss her. Gaby had been with him for a long time. That was all.

He was used to her. He hated the thought of training someone else.

Who the fuck was he kidding? He couldn't imagine his life without her. He sat back on his heels, stunned and a bit frightened at the thought. Gabrielle was in every part of his life. It would be brutal to pull her out of it. He shook his head.

"I haven't spent three years with you on a lark. We work well together. The sex is good. I don't see why we can't continue for the foreseeable future."

"But you don't love me," she said quietly. This time, he could tell it wasn't a question. "You're not ever going to fall in love with me. If three years of living with me hasn't done it, it's not going to happen."

Cal put his hands on her shoulders. He forced her to look into his eyes. Why the hell was she pushing him? What did she think she was going to get out of this? "I never promised to be anything more than your Master."

The tears in her eyes almost did him in, but he forced himself to hold her apart. She would use any weakness against him.

She brushed a hand over her cheeks, whisking the tears away. The pain in her eyes—that stayed right where it was. "You were honest, Callum. I was fooling myself. Could you leave me alone for a moment? I'd like to get dressed."

"Gabrielle, it's one in the morning." He stared at the gold choker around her throat that marked her as his submissive. He didn't use the word slave, though it practically described her. She never argued with him, never fought. She did exactly what he told her to do and he was counting on that fact now. "You're going to bed. In the morning, we'll get back to normal."

For the first time in their three years together, she shook her head, indicating her negative response.

He watched with shock as her hands went behind her neck. She unclasped the necklace she'd worn without fail for years. Eyes downcast, she offered it back to him.

"I'm sure you'll need it for the next one." She forced the necklace into his hand, her eyes lingering on it briefly before she looked up at him. Her politeness held a brittle edge. "My suitcase is already packed. If you'll give me a moment to get dressed, I'll leave."

He felt his face harden, jaw tightening as he realized what was really happening. She was going all out with this one. She thought she could pull a power play on him? He wouldn't be manipulated, and perhaps it was time to show her who held all the cards in this game she'd started. "Explain to me how you intend to leave? My name is on that car of yours. All of your credit cards are in my name as well. And your bank account."

She flushed, a sure sign that he'd hurt her. Well, she'd hurt him, too. Her eyes narrowed on him. She was absolutely gorgeous when she was angry. Her green eyes were darker, and her sable hair flowed across her shoulders. Everything about Gabrielle was soft and feminine. Even in her rage, she brought out his protective instincts. He fought to ignore them.

"I believe it was in our contract, Callum. If I stayed for at least two years, I'd get to keep the car, and you owe me fifty thousand dollars. Maybe I earned it on my back, but I earned it."

"Oh, but you weren't merely on your back, were you, sweetheart?" Cal could hear the ugly edge to his voice but did nothing to temper it. "You were on your front, your knees, tied up, tied down, however I liked it."

"Yes, it was however you liked it. I did everything you asked me to do."

He hated the fact that she wouldn't fight with him. It made him crazy. It made him cruel. "I remember distinctly you arguing with me about that contract. You told me to pull the monetary clauses out because you didn't need them."

"I was wrong."

He shook his head, unwilling to continue the game a second longer. He had her in check. "You can try to enforce that contract, darlin'. I can keep you tied up in court for a really long time. You'll be an old woman before you see a dime of that money."

Her beautiful face lost every bit of its color. The blood drained from her complexion so quickly Cal worried she might pass out.

"You won't give me the money? I thought you would honor the contract. I didn't think you would turn me out with nothing."

He nearly growled his frustration. "I'm not turning you out. You're threatening to leave because your plans to manipulate me didn't work. I'm not giving you a dime. You can forget that plan, get back into bed, and in the morning, we'll pretend this never happened. I'm willing to be magnanimous."

He watched as she seemed to be seeking a way out. There wasn't one. He was right. She wouldn't try to enforce the contract they had signed at the beginning of the relationship. It was a BDSM contract with all sorts of boundaries. She would never take it to another lawyer. He was the best lawyer in Fort Worth. He knew exactly how to get out of his contract with Gabrielle.

She took a long breath. "I'll find another way. I can get a job or something."

Cal thought she said it more to herself than to him.

She glanced up at him. "If you don't mind stepping out, I need to get dressed. I'll call Heather. She can come and get me. Feel free to look through the suitcase. I'm only taking the things I came here with. You can donate the clothes and stuff to charity or find another plump girl to take my place."

"Gabrielle!" He used his Dom voice on her, the one that told her

16

she had some punishment coming.

"You can't spank me anymore. I took off my collar." She sighed and got up, pulling the sheet with her. She wound it around her body, covering it from him. She walked to the bathroom, obviously tired of waiting for him to give her the privacy she requested. "I can think whatever I want, do whatever I like. I'm not your responsibility anymore."

That statement hit him squarely in the gut. She'd been his responsibility for years. How could she just take off the collar he'd placed on her? She'd given it back like it meant nothing. Like they'd meant nothing.

A memory of the night he'd placed that collar around her neck played through his head like a movie he couldn't look away from.

They'd been private about it. Some of their friends had ceremonies at the various clubs they attended, but it seemed too close to marriage for Cal to feel comfortable. Instead he'd taken her to Austin, wined and dined her, and gently put the collar on when they got back to their suite.

She'd been naked and flushed, her hair all around her like some lush fertility goddess, and when she'd looked up at him, his collar around her neck, he'd felt something he'd never felt before in his life.

Right. He'd felt right.

He'd made love to her for hours that night.

He still felt right with her. How was she walking away? Had it all been an illusion?

He grabbed her arm and hauled her around to face him. "Why the hell did you stay with me for three years, Gabrielle? Because you thought I would marry you?"

She touched his face with her free hand, her fingers slipping slowly over his cheeks and down his jaw. It was a gentle caress, long and steady, as though she were trying to memorize the feeling. "No. I think I always knew you wouldn't love me. I was fooling myself. But that wasn't why I stayed. I stayed with you because *I* love *you*, Cal."

He wanted…fuck he didn't know what he wanted anymore. She had him chasing his own tail at this point. "But you don't love me anymore?"

She shook her head. "I love you. I'll always love you. It just isn't enough. I want to be loved, too. I want someone to love me the way you loved Cassie. Don't I deserve that?"

He dropped her arm, unable to look at her a moment longer. The door behind him closed, and he sank to the bed, head in his hands.

He couldn't, wouldn't love Gabrielle. He would never allow another woman inside his heart like that. It hurt too much. He could still see Cassie's body lying on a cold slab in the morgue. She'd been thirty-two years old. He couldn't love another woman.

His heart hurt, the ache making him touch his chest to make sure he hadn't started bleeding. The pain…fuck, he'd promised himself he wouldn't feel this kind of pain again.

Gabrielle was right. She did deserve better.

Like a robot, he forced himself to stand, forced opened the drawer of his desk and took out his checkbook. His hand shook slightly as he wrote out the check, adding another ten grand to the total. He found the title to the BMW and signed it over to her. He would call Heather and have everything he'd bought Gabrielle shipped to her new address.

He wouldn't take another sub. He couldn't imagine wanting anyone else.

Gabrielle looked older when she emerged from the bathroom. She wore faded jeans and a black shirt. He hated when she wore black. She thought it was slimming, but she didn't need to be slimmed. She had an hourglass figure. He loved her curves. Her breasts were large and real. They matched her luscious hips and that ass he couldn't get enough of. She was perfect. Her head was high as she reached for the bag she'd hidden away in the closet.

"Good-bye, Callum," she said quietly. "I hope you find someone you can love someday."

He pressed the paperwork in her hand. Her eyes flared briefly, but she thanked him, as though she were accepting a small courtesy, not taking the outcome of years of their relationship. He forced himself to be as cold as ice. If he didn't, he'd be on his knees begging her not to leave.

"Good-bye, Gabrielle."

She walked into the night.

And he was alone again.

Chapter One

Ten months later

Callum stared at her, not quite believing his eyes. He stood in the elegant living room of Greg and Heather Hall's large house in North Dallas and watched the woman holding court by the pool. The French doors that led from the living room out to the backyard were open, and he couldn't mistake that laugh. The house was full and the party had spilled out into the warm night.

She was out there. Gabrielle. He couldn't believe the change. His shy pet was the life of the party. Every man in the place was looking at his former submissive.

He didn't blame them. No hetero man could miss those tits. They were rounder and higher than they'd been almost a year before. No way to miss the change in them. It hadn't been brought on by exercise. No those sweet things had been surgically enhanced.

He could actually feel his blood pressure rising. How much of the money he'd given her had gone toward her boob job? The ten months they'd spent apart had brought about several changes in Gabrielle. Along with the vivacious personality and the tits of steel, she'd cut her long, luxurious hair. It was ridiculously short now, a boyish cut. He'd insisted she wear it long, down to her waist. He had loved the way it flowed down her back.

Had she cut it to spite him? An act of rebellion against the man she hadn't been able to control?

"Cal?" A soft voice cut through ever-darkening thoughts. "I wasn't expecting you."

He had to force himself to turn from Gabrielle in order to pay attention to his hostess. Heather Hall was a tall, willowy blonde. Her model-perfect looks were moving past worried and into full-on panic. He managed to give her a little smile. What was going on in her head to have her look so worried? "Have I ever missed Greg's birthday?"

"You were supposed to be in Atlanta."

Perhaps seeing Gabrielle after all this time was unnerving him, but he would have sworn he detected a note of accusation in her tone.

He shrugged and turned his attention back to Gabrielle. She laughed at something a big, dark-haired man said, the sound practically musical to his ears. Had she ever laughed like that when they'd been together, a laugh of complete, unselfconscious joy? She leaned in toward the other, her hand coming out to touch his shoulder. Cal had the sudden urge to beat the shit out of the stranger.

"I was told you would be in Atlanta for at least another couple of days. You didn't RSVP," Heather continued.

Yes, there was all kinds of accusations there. "I'm sorry about the RSVP. I absolutely should have. As for not being in Atlanta, I got the deal closed early. All of Greg's paperwork is done. He's thrilled with the terms I managed to negotiate."

Greg Hall was one of the country's up-and-coming hotel magnates. His line of boutique and specialty hotels had made him a fortune and brought Cal an enormous amount of business.

"More than thrilled." Greg walked up behind his wife. He looked Heather straight in the eyes. "Is there a reason you're being ridiculously rude to Callum, dear?"

Cal nearly smiled at the deep tone his best friend's voice suddenly took on. It sent Heather's eyes submissively down. Her mouth became a flat line, her shoulders rigid. That was one pissed off sub. He needed to remember to ask his secretary to keep track of his social engagements because apparently Heather was serious about the RSVP. She kept her composure, though. She apologized and went to check on the caterer.

"I'll add that to her list of punishments," Greg said with a half smile. "She can rack up the punishment time when she gets going.

Our marriage wouldn't work if she wasn't a tiny bit of a masochist."

He couldn't do the small talk thing right now and he couldn't worry about social niceties. Now that he really thought it through, he had to consider that Heather had planned this party specifically for a day he was supposed to be out of town. Had she done that for Gabrielle?

"What's Gabrielle doing here?"

It had been almost a year, and he hadn't heard a word from her or about her. He found it hard to believe that it was a coincidence she showed up to a party he shouldn't have been able to attend.

"It's my birthday party." Greg took a swig of his imported beer. "I think Heather invited everyone we know. She's Heather's best friend, and she happened to be in town. Are you two going to have a problem?"

Callum frowned. Greg was staring at him with a bland, but slightly distasteful look. It was the expression he tended to have on his face when dealing with people he didn't want to deal with. What had happened to put that look on his best friend's face? Then again, how long had it been since he'd called Greg about anything besides business? It had been before he and Gaby had broken up. Had it really been ten months since he'd spent time with his friend? He had allowed this thing with Gabrielle to affect him far too much. He gave Greg a friendly smile. "Not at all. I was simply surprised to see her. I assure you I have no interest in speaking to Gabrielle."

Greg's eyes got flat and cold. "It's best that you don't. It would upset Heather, and I wouldn't appreciate it. If you can't get along with her, you should leave. Let me know if you need anything and enjoy the party."

He stared as Greg walked away. What the hell had that been about? Actually, now that he thought about it, everyone had been a bit chilly around him lately. He looked around the elegantly decorated room and felt the weight of judgmental eyes on him. What exactly were they judging him for?

Gabrielle laughed brightly and he knew. This was her revenge. New hair. New body. New stories and rumors about her nasty, mean old Master. What exactly had she told his friends?

Disappointment racked through him. He would give it to her. She knew where to hit him. He hated gossip about himself, loathed the idea of people talking about him, so this was an excellent revenge. He wasn't a terribly social person so turning the small number of friends he did have against him would certainly strike a blow.

He hadn't expected that of her. She'd been sweet and thoughtful. She'd been the kind of woman who was always kind, even when she probably shouldn't be. Had it all been one big lie to try to get him to marry her? A knot of bitterness twisted inside him. He'd been mooning over her while she'd been getting a boob job and bitching behind his back.

If she thought he would let her get away with it for one moment, she had never known him at all.

* * * *

Gabrielle knew the minute her day went to complete hell. She felt his eyes on her, the instinct of a poor prey animal in the midst of a predator. Every nerve in her body turned on like someone had flipped a switch. She tried not to look at him, but her eyes kept finding his tall, muscular form.

Cal stood in the middle of the crowd but there was no question that he was alone. He was a man who held himself apart.

"Is there a problem, love?"

She looked up at the gorgeous Irishman Heather had introduced her to earlier. Lee something. He was working security for the party. She'd found him very interesting. Naturally she was in the midst of millionaires and billionaires and the one man she truly enjoyed talking to was working.

They had a lot in common. He was working for a start-up security firm. She was starting up again. With everything…

She shook her head. "No, just someone I hoped to avoid."

His eyes went cold and she suddenly believed his stories about working for Irish intelligence. "Would you like to point him out to me? Getting rid of problems is why I'm here."

She rather thought he was here simply to ensure nothing went wrong around Greg's ultra-rich clients and friends. It wouldn't do him a lot of good to bounce Greg's longtime best friend out of his party simply because she was uncomfortable.

She shook her head. "Not at all. He's an ex. We parted amicably. But it is the first time I've seen him since we broke up."

Amicably might be stretching it, but in the end they'd parted per the terms of the contract they'd begun the relationship with. Once Cal had realized she wasn't going to stay, he'd backed off and honored the paperwork they'd signed. He hadn't tried to call her afterward or follow-up to see how she was doing, and a part of her had been grateful.

Did he have a new sub? He seemed to be alone here but then he'd never required her to hover around him at a party.

"Ah," the Irishman said. "That can be difficult. If you want some advice from me—and I'm sure you don't—get it over with. Say hello. Talk to the man and you'll probably discover he's feeling as awkward as you are."

Somehow she doubted that, but she still couldn't stop herself from looking back at him. He was shaking his head at the server offering him a drink.

God, that was a beautiful man. She'd missed him so much over the past eight months.

The Irishman touched the small device in his ear. "Yes, I hear ya. I'll check it out, Alex." He smiled down at her and Gaby wished she was over Cal because that man was stunning. "We've got a couple of photographers walking around outside. Time for me to show them the door. Good luck with him. If you ask me, there's probably a lot to talk about between the two of you. No one looks quite that long at a man she's over. Nice to meet you, Gaby."

He walked away and Gaby sought a quiet part of the yard. She lingered at the edge of the pool, hoping Cal didn't notice her. The hot Irish guy's words were playing through her head. Was she over him? It had been months since she'd even thought about sex, but the second she realized Callum Reed was in the same room, her hormones started singing a chorus.

"I'm sorry, sweetie," Heather whispered, walking up to her and giving her a big hug. "I had no idea Cal was going to show. Apparently, he finished up the deal in Atlanta early. I'll be honest, I didn't expect him to come even if he didn't have a deal to work on.

23

He's been completely MIA for months."

"He hasn't been going to the club?" She couldn't imagine Callum not spending time at the small fetish club he'd helped to start. It was where they had first met. It was where they had first made love.

It was where he'd first fucked her. She had to be real. Fooling herself had merely gotten her in trouble. Callum Reed had loved one woman in his life, and it wasn't her.

Heather looked thoughtful as she took a sip of her margarita. "He's only come in once in the last couple of months. He had a Scotch, walked the dungeon, and then went home. Alone. I expected him to start going through a sub a night the way he did before he met you, but as far as I can tell, he's been alone."

She seriously doubted he'd been alone. She snuck a glance his way. He looked gorgeous in his designer suit. It was black with pinstripes and fit him perfectly. He had them done by an Italian tailor, picking them up once a year when he went to Milan on business.

She smoothed her shaking hands over the dove-gray dress she'd bought for thirty-nine ninety-nine at a discount store. When she'd been with Cal, it had been designer clothes all the way. Of course, she hadn't been paying for all those clothes. Or the house, or the car.

She paid for everything now, and everything had become decidedly bargain basement. Despite the nice salary Greg paid her to run his island resort, she had racked up some massive bills. It would be a while before she picked up any luxuries.

"I'm sure he's been discreet. He hasn't been celibate." Callum Reed wasn't capable of celibacy. He was the kind of man who needed sex at least twice a day. He'd take it as often as he could get it, of course, but twice a day was his absolute minimum.

When they'd been together, he would wake her up every morning, his hard cock poking her in the backside. He would roll her over and thrust inside before she was even awake. Other times, he would work warm lube into her ass before spreading her cheeks and pushing into her tight hole. Morning was quick and hard. Night was long and languid. He could play with her for hours. Sometimes she thought he viewed oral sex the way some people watched television.

"Don't let him ruin the party for you," Heather practically pleaded. "You have to go back to the island tomorrow and I'll miss

24

you again."

She would miss Heather, too. Heather had been a rock for the last hellacious year of Gaby's life. No matter how bad it had gotten, Heather had been there, holding her hand. "It's only for a few weeks. You'll be out at the resort in June. Greg has big plans for your anniversary. I'll make sure to have the handcuffs shiny for you."

"Oh, honey, I always bring my own." Heather winked at her. She glanced up as though she suddenly remembered her duties as hostess. "I have to mingle. I saw you talking to that gorgeous security guy. Word of warning—the rumor is he's a player. Greg hired this new security firm and, holy hell, they're all gorgeous and super alpha, but from what I can tell, they're also crazy. You need a serious man. I'll introduce you to my doctor friend before dinner. He's a keeper, dear. A Dom looking for a permanent sub."

"Yeah, I've heard that before." She smiled weakly as Heather walked off to mingle with her husband's friends and clients. Gaby was left clutching a half-filled margarita glass. She shrugged and made it an empty margarita glass. A pleasant warmth started in her belly.

Going ten months without liquor made her a cheap date. That could change now. She wasn't under the same restrictions. When she got back to work, she would start going to happy hour with her staff. It had been long enough. It was time. She stared up at the night sky. Though the stars weren't as brilliant as they were in her new home, it was still beautiful, brilliant jewels in a canopy of the darkest velvet.

She was here and it *was* time. It was time to grow out her hair and drink some martinis and meet a new man. She took a deep breath. It was time to start living again.

"Gabrielle."

The urge to drop to her knees was right there, the impulse a result of years of careful training. It was hard to ignore, but she turned and looked at the man she had loved enough to walk away from.

"Hello, Cal," she said evenly. "How are you?"

He looked her up and down, his dark blue eyes showing absolutely no expression. Those eyes assessed her, roaming every inch of her body in a decidedly clinical fashion. "I've been perfectly fine, Gabrielle. How have you been?"

His hand was suddenly on her elbow. Her skin tingled where he touched her. He didn't pull at her, merely squeezed gently, and she let him lead her. Yes, that was a force of habit, too, but perhaps her Irish friend was right. If they had any hopes of being comfortable around each other, they had to talk. They began walking slowly away from the pool.

"I'm well." That could have come out a little stronger. She sounded like a scared rabbit and that wasn't at all the impression she wanted to make on Cal.

"That's nice." Naturally, his voice sounded perfectly even. He could be negotiating a deal rather than talking to an old lover. "From the evil glances I'm getting from some very old friends, I would think I had tried to kill you."

"I'm sorry, what?" This wasn't the way she'd expected their first meeting to go. She'd kind of avoided thinking about it.

His jaw went tight. "I'm talking about all my friends looking at me like I'm some kind of criminal. I'll admit I haven't exactly been social lately, but I didn't expect to walk into a party and find myself completely unwelcome. The only thing that's changed is the status of our relationship, so I'm wondering what's been said about me."

Damn Heather and her big mouth. It was supposed to be a secret. She smiled brightly and slipped her arm through Cal's. Yes, she needed to handle this. She'd never intended to make anyone hate Cal. He simply hadn't been able to love her.

She had no interest in the two of them becoming a focus of gossip. If she seemed comfortable with her ex-lover, perhaps the other guests wouldn't talk about them. She tried to look nonchalant. "I have no idea why. I haven't seen any of these people since I left town ten months ago. Maybe it's me they're wary of."

"I doubt that, pet," Cal said, all silky and smooth. His voice had a direct line to her soft parts. "Even my oldest friend seems to have turned on me. Greg barely spoke to me this evening. His friendliest words were to tell me to leave you alone. I swear, Gabrielle, if he didn't need me to broker his deals, he might not talk to me at all. Now I wonder why that is."

Gaby flushed, guilt flooding her system. She truly hadn't meant to hurt him, but she didn't want to rehash the end of their relationship.

She'd kept the secret this long. There was no reason he should know about it now. "I don't know. I have never spoken to Greg about us."

"I'm sure Heather talks enough."

Gaby felt her heels sink into the grass as they left the deck. The evening grew darker as the lights from the torches got further away. The gazebo in the distance seemed to be Cal's destination. She followed willingly. If they were going to talk, it was best to do it in private.

"I can't control Heather's mouth. That's supposed to be Greg's job. He's her husband, after all."

Cal helped her up the gazebo's steps. He was always solicitous. It was one of the first things to attract her. He was a Dom of the first order. Gaby had been looking for someone like Callum since the day she realized there was a whole world out there for people like her. She'd gone through a couple of men who claimed to be Doms but really just used it as an excuse to be selfish. A real Dominant was someone like Cal, who always took care of her, even if he didn't love her.

"Well, as it was pointed out to me recently, a Dom only has as much control as his sub allows him." His deep blue eyes were almost black in the moonlight and there were lines around them that hadn't been there before. There was a weariness to his frame that called to her. She fought the urge to smooth down his tie and snuggle in his arms. He wasn't hers to take care of anymore. He turned to her. "So what have you been up to since you left?"

Her hand unconsciously went to her breast, thinking of the pain that centered there. "This and that."

He leaned back, staring at her as though trying to decide something. "I never could figure you out, Gabrielle. I didn't know if you were simply content to be kept or if there was some ambition lurking under the placid surface."

The darkness was a welcome ally as she felt herself flush. If they'd been under even the soft lights of the party, he would have known how much that hurt. "Well, you weren't interested in my ambitions."

He shrugged. "I just wondered what you did all day."

Her laugh was bitter and without an ounce of humor. "I ate

bonbons and watched soaps. I counted the hours until you got home."
She turned away from him and looked out over the yard. In the
distance, her friends mingled and laughed. She still seemed so far
away from them. Maybe she would always seem far away now.

Distance had given her some perspective, especially when it
came to her old Dom. "You weren't interested in who I was as a
person, Callum. You were interested in who I was as a sub. My
submissive self was docile and sweet. That was what mattered to you.
I didn't ask questions or make demands. It was a D/s relationship. It
wasn't a love affair."

She knew the difference now.

His fingers ran across the exposed skin of her shoulders and she
held on to the railing of the gazebo. The spaghetti straps that held her
dress up offered little protection against his gentle assault. She
shivered at the touch.

"And you don't want that anymore, do you? You don't want a
man to dominate you? You don't want a man to take charge?"

Oh, there were certainly parts of her that did. His hands ran down
to her waist, settling on her hips. *Push him away. Do it now or this is
going to go poorly. You are not capable of handling this.*

But she'd waited too long. When he pressed his groin against her
backside, she could feel the hard ridge of his erection, and she knew
she wasn't going to walk away.

It was only sex. Sex with Callum had been mind-blowingly good.
There wasn't any reason she couldn't enjoy it again as long as she
held herself apart. It had been so long. And tomorrow morning, she
would be on a flight back to her island, where she was surrounded by
gorgeous men she couldn't fuck because they were either an
employee or a guest. She was starting over. Shouldn't she honor her
past with one last nice night?

Yeah, her girl parts were super stupid and they were firmly in
control.

Cal pressed his hard dick against her and her brain no longer
mattered. That dick had been the best she'd ever had and her whole
body reacted. It was like her body knew what it had been through in
the last ten months and was demanding payment. That big, hard dick
was payment for all the pain.

She could handle it. Hell, after what she'd been through, she could handle anything.

"I didn't say I wasn't interested in a Dominant man," she heard herself saying in a deep, seductive voice she didn't quite recognize.

He chuckled behind her, his breath warm against the back of her neck. "I didn't think so, pet. You always did love the dirty stuff. It's hard to believe a woman as submissive as you could really walk away from it altogether. Do you have a new Dom, Gabrielle?"

"No." She was barely managing to breathe. His hands moved up her torso. He cupped her breasts, seeming to weigh and learn their new contours. She stilled, trying to figure out what to say if he asked about the obvious changes there. She wished so much she was still sensitive. She used to love the feel of his hands on her breasts.

"Why not, baby? You love this." It sounded almost like an accusation, but Gaby was too busy rubbing her ass against his cock to really register the menace in his voice. There was a distant alarm bell going off in the background of her brain, but she ignored it. She wanted, no, needed, what only Cal had ever been able to give her.

"Gabrielle," he said in that dark voice of his, "get on your knees."

She turned and complied, shutting her brain off. This wasn't a place to listen to reason. This was that glorious place where she simply listened to Callum. He would take care of her. He always did. She dropped to her knees, the hard wood of the gazebo merely another sensation to be had.

"You know what I want, pet."

His voice was seduction in and of itself. She couldn't refuse him when he used that tone on her. Her hands trembled as she undid his belt and unbuttoned his slacks. It didn't matter that anyone could walk up on them. That thought just made her wetter. It felt good to want something. His big cock sprang free as she pushed his boxers out of the way. She sighed as she saw the pearly drop already leaking from the slit of his dick. She couldn't help herself. Her tongue came out. She ran it across his head, gathering the pre-cum. It was salty on her tongue. She wanted more. She lightly pulled the head of his cock into her mouth, milking him gently for the salty stuff.

This was what she needed. Closure. Or hell, maybe not. Maybe she could see him when she came into town. Callum was a treat. He was dessert. She didn't have to have him all the time, but life was useless if she never indulged again.

Who the fuck was she fooling?

"Damn it, Gabrielle," he growled. "Suck me."

His hands came down, tangling in what was left of her hair. She briefly bemoaned its loss. The new pixie cut was chic, but she'd only gotten it out of necessity. She remembered how Cal loved her long hair. He would wrap it around his fist and gently direct her. Now, he struggled to get a hold of it. He managed and pushed his cock into her mouth as he pulled at her head.

She let her tongue whirl around his silky, hard shaft, relearning the shape and feel of him. She let him guide her, sucking hard along him. He pushed her, tunneling his way to the back of her throat, then groaned as she fought to keep him inside. She hollowed out her cheeks when he tried to pull out.

"God, you give the best head," he muttered. "No one ever came close, but then you were always the best at everything."

She turned her eyes up. He was looking down, watching his cock fuck her mouth. His eyes were hot as he peered down. His hips thrust forward. She checked her gag reflex and concentrated on breathing through her nose. She reached up and rolled his tight balls in her hands. He hissed, the sound pushing out between his teeth. She'd heard it so many times and knew exactly what it meant. He was close, so close. His cock swelled in the already tight confines of her mouth. It was only seconds before he would come. She couldn't wait. When he was done, it would be her turn. He would pull off her panties and arrange her on the bench. He would spread her legs and feast on her pussy. It would feel so good.

"I'm going to come, pet," he announced softly but with purpose. "That tight mouth of yours is too much. You'll swallow me. Don't you dare lose a drop."

She would have smiled if she hadn't had a mouthful of urgent cock. As if she would do anything else. She softened her throat. Callum groaned as she swallowed around him. He'd described it once as a soft, sweet vise around his dick. It was different than her pussy or her ass. The sound of Cal's moan filled the gazebo and rolled over her, filling her with an erotic pride. He might not have loved her, but

30

he'd always made her feel wanted. The first hot jet of Cal's cum spurted onto her tongue. The taste was familiar, and Gaby heard her own throaty sounds as she struggled to push him as far as he could go. Gaby swallowed, not wanting to miss a drop. She sucked him while he softened. He pulled out of her mouth with a soft pop.

She sat back on her heels, a little surprised. She drew in the humid air, struggling to catch her breath. Usually, he wanted her to lick him clean. It was a soft time she craved, the time where they connected on a non-physical level. He would stroke her hair while she ran her tongue along him. He would tell her how much he enjoyed her, how pretty she was. She would cling to him and they would kiss for what felt like hours, tasting his salty essence on her own tongue. They would stroke and play all night, his deep voice praising her.

He said nothing now, merely tucked his cock in and zipped up his pants. He stepped back, not even lending a hand to get her off her knees. What was happening? A chill started to push through the warmth of before. She pushed up against the bench to get herself into a standing position because she suddenly felt like she needed every inch of height she had to face him down.

She had made a terrible mistake.

"Thanks, sweetheart." Cal's voice made a mockery of the quiet surroundings, pulling her out of their intimacy. "How much do I owe you for the hummer?"

"What?" It was penetrating her brain that he'd used her with no thought to making it mutual. He didn't look like a man who was about to repay the favor.

His sensual lips looked a little cruel in the low light. "The blow job, Gabrielle. How much? I think I have a fifty on me. I know you don't fuck me for fun."

"I thought…" She let the sentence dangle as humiliation swept over her body.

A low laugh cut through her like a knife meant to tear her apart.

"What? Did you think I wanted to fuck you, baby? Did you think I'd take care of you now? I have it on the highest authority that I'm no longer responsible for your orgasms. You have some fingers. Take care of yourself. Or you could ask that asshole you were talking to earlier. Maybe you can get a ring out of him." He winked at her. It

31

was an ugly thing.

The nice Irish guy who had told her she needed to deal with Cal. She didn't think this was what he'd meant. She felt Cal stare at her, and her skin chilled under his cold appraisal.

"I don't want to fuck you, Gabrielle. I'm afraid this new look you've come up with isn't attractive. The boobs are bigger, but I can't stand silicone and you know that. The hair is terrible, and you're far too thin for my tastes."

She touched her hair and felt the tears cloud her vision. Her hair had only started growing back a few months before. She'd been bald for so long, she'd worried it wouldn't grow back at all.

Oh, god, she'd been right to leave him. If he thought she looked bad now, he wouldn't have been able to look at her when it had been bad. He wouldn't have stuck around anyway. She wobbled on her heels. It didn't matter. His cruel words had cured her of any lingering desire for him. She'd never been anything to him but a convenient lay and a cheap housekeeper. He couldn't treat her the way he had if he'd ever cared about her. She patted her hair down, trying to regain some semblance of dignity.

Suddenly she wondered if he knew and didn't care. After all, Heather loved to talk. He had to have heard, but she was going to make sure.

"Sorry you don't like it, Callum," she managed with as much bravado as she could muster. "You should have seen it a couple of months back. You would have loved it then. As for my skinny body, well, I found the best diet ever. Chemo will get you to your goal weight in a hurry. Keep your money. I'll consider the blow job a life lesson. Good-bye."

"Gaby?"

He so rarely called her by anything but her full name that this nearly made her stop. And then she remembered her name meant nothing to him. She was nothing to him.

She walked away from him, holding her head high when the need to hide herself away was riding her hard. Tears pulsed at her eyes, but she wasn't shedding them. Not yet. She strode past the pool, ignoring the people who greeted her. She got her purse and went straight out to her car without saying good-bye to her hosts. It was rude, but she couldn't face anyone now. She started the car just as Cal caught up to her.

"Gabrielle!"

Even inside the car, she could hear the command in his voice. She pulled away, the tires screeching against the pavement. She didn't owe him anything. All their debts had been paid and there had never honestly been anything but a contract between them. Gaby felt the sadness well up inside her as she drove off. There was nothing between them now, not even friendship. In the morning, she would get on a plane and leave him behind again.

It was time to go home.

* * * *

Cal strode back into Greg's house knowing full well he looked like an angry bull. Fucking confused bull was what he really was. He wanted very desperately to gore someone, but he had no idea where to charge.

People all around him quickly moved to get out of his way. He thought briefly about getting into his Jag and pursuing her but changed his mind. It was obvious that a lot had been kept from him. He needed to know what had been going on. Greg knew. That son of a bitch knew and hadn't bothered to mention it to him.

He stood there like an asshole, watching her POS car drive off.

What had happened? Chemo? What sort of cancer had she lived through? His heart thudded in his chest, and the room seemed to squeeze around him. She'd been too thin and he'd made fun of her. He'd fucking made fun of her when she was hurting and healing and…god, he was an ass of the highest order. How long had she had…he couldn't say it, even think it. Had she known when she left him?

Across the room, he saw Greg laughing at something Heather said. Anger flooded Cal's system. He welcomed it. Anger was easier to deal with than the fear and guilt that had crushed him from the moment Gaby had smoothed down her hair and made her announcement. His stomach was in knots. Beating the shit out of Greg would make him feel infinitely more in control.

Greg looked up, regarding him with a little bit of disdain in his eyes. That disdain was quickly replaced with startled shock as Cal bore down on him. Cal was satisfied at the way Greg's eyes widened and he quickly set his beer down and pushed Heather out of the way. He looked at Cal like he probably would look at a snarling dog. His hands came up, wary, worried. "Cal, whatever is going through your brain, we should talk about it."

"Fuck talking," he spat out as his fist connected with Greg's jaw. The sight of Greg hitting the floor satisfied Cal deeply.

"Goddamn it." Greg picked himself up. He rubbed his jaw. All around them people looked on in shock. Heather pushed at Cal, her manicured nails shoving at him.

"You asshole. Get out of my house," she swore.

He looked down at the woman he'd known for ten years. He'd introduced her to her husband. Now she looked at him like he was a monster. It didn't matter. All that mattered was figuring out what had happened. It suddenly seemed like he hadn't ever known the answer to that question.

"I'm not going anywhere until someone explains what the hell is wrong with Gabrielle."

Heather's eyes turned down. Cal knew her well enough. A small suspicion started in the back of his brain. He turned to Greg, who pulled his wife out of the line of fire. Greg wouldn't see it. All he would see was another Dom intruding on his territory.

"I think you should leave now, Callum." Greg's voice was stony and flat.

Cal held his ground. He wasn't going anywhere until he got what he needed. He had to make himself intensely plain. "I told you. I'm not leaving until you explain why Gaby needed fucking chemotherapy. Don't pretend. I know you know."

Greg ran a hand over his jaw. "Of course I know. Who do you think paid for her reconstructive surgery?"

"What?" The minute the words registered, Cal felt his knees buckle and had to force himself to keep standing. The world had tilted, and he didn't like where he landed.

Surgery? Reconstruction? What had she been through?

Fuck. What had she been through without him?

"Holy shit, Cal." Greg put an arm on Cal's shoulder to steady him. The wary, almost disdainful look that had been on Greg's face was replaced with an expression of confusion. "Are you telling me you didn't know?"

He felt his jaw firm into granite. God, he was going to throw up. His stomach was churning. Where was the bathroom?

Luckily he'd been here before and knew where to run. He slammed through the door and hit his knees.

Gabrielle. His Gabrielle had been cut on, drugs poured through her system, and she'd been alone. She'd fucking been alone. And the first time he'd seen her, he'd insulted her and taken from her.

It all came up. Oddly, he wouldn't have thought there would be that much. He didn't eat a lot anymore, didn't have the will since she'd left him.

He was shaking when he heard the voices behind him.

"Cal, are you all right?"

No wonder they all looked at him like he was a fucking monster. He *was*. He was the piece of shit Dom who hadn't even noticed his sub was dying.

Cal fell back, his spine hitting the wall of the guest bathroom with a resounding thud, and he let his head fall forward. All he had left was his reputation. It appeared even that was tarnished beyond belief. "Do you honestly believe I would have allowed her to go through that alone? I might be a son of a bitch, but I have always cared for my sub. I took care of Gabrielle."

"Not enough to marry her." Heather stood next to her husband and it was obvious Cal's sacrificial stomach wasn't enough for her.

Greg turned to his wife, his jaw tightening. "You made me believe he knew what was happening with Gaby and that he didn't care. You have a lot of explaining to do. Don't look at me that way. This isn't some small rebellion. This is you coming between me and my oldest friend. This is very serious."

"I never lied to you, Master," Heather said stubbornly. It was easy to see she was flustered. She'd used her husband's title at a decidedly vanilla party.

Greg stepped into the bathroom, offering a hand up. He took it, getting shakily to his feet.

"Cal, if you would join me in the office, I think we should

conclude this in private. Heather, see to our guests." His voice went low and he leaned in. "I will handle you later, slave. It will not go well for you."

Cal rinsed his mouth out, washing cold water over his face before he left the bathroom.

Greg stalked through the crowd. Cal forced himself to follow, making his limbs move like they were machines. Greg knew. Did know. Had known. He knew what had happened all those months before.

Gaby's pale face haunted him. He'd used her ruthlessly, wanting to pay her back for every restless night he'd had since she left him. He could hear his cold words, each one calculated to hurt her. Every single syllable an arrow he'd launched in a battle she hadn't been fighting. Shame made his shoulders droop, his body feel like he wasn't in it. He sank into the soft leather of the sofa as Greg closed the door behind him. Cal tried to steady his shaking hands as Greg quickly poured him a couple of fingers of Scotch. The single malt burned a path to his gut.

Greg's head shook as he took his own drink. "I can't begin to tell you how sorry I am, man. All this time, I thought you knew."

"Will you tell me what the fuck I'm supposed to know? Give it to me straight." He took another long swallow. He had the feeling he would need it.

Greg sat down and looked Cal in the eye. There was no anger left, only a weary sadness. "Eleven months ago, Gaby was diagnosed with stage two breast cancer."

Cal's hand tightened around the glass so he wouldn't drop it. He knew her family history. Gabrielle's mother had died of breast cancer when she was just sixteen. Because of her family history, she got a mammogram every year despite her youth. He'd teased her about it, saying something about how sensitive her breasts were. He'd allowed her to go alone because he'd had some meeting.

She must have been terrified when she'd gotten the news. He hated the thought that she had been alone. He should have been by her side. He let his head fall forward as Greg continued to talk.

"It had spread to her lymph nodes. It was an aggressive strain. Given her family history with it, the doctors recommended she have a bilateral mastectomy. She refused at first. It was only in one breast."

Cal's head came up. He felt a moment's pure panic. "Tell me she did what the doctors told her to do. Tell me they took both of those things off her body."

He'd loved her breasts, adored lavishing them with affection, but in a moment they'd become the enemy. They threatened to take her out of the world and they needed to be gone.

Greg nodded, leaning forward. "Heather talked her into it. It was a really bad time. Gaby was worried no one would want her after the surgery. She was a little lost. You had just broken up with her."

He laughed but it was a bitter thing. "Is that what she told you? I didn't break up with her, Greg. It wasn't a thought in my head. I was happy. I was gloriously happy until the night she walked out on me. I got completely blindsided. She gave me an ultimatum. I had to tell her I loved her and would marry her or she would leave. You know how I deal with ultimatums. Did she tell you I kicked her out?"

Greg rolled his eyes, obviously angry with himself. "No. She never said that. Heather never said it either. She simply didn't correct my mistaken impression. I couldn't imagine that she would leave you. Gaby loved you so much. I could see it in her eyes when she looked at you."

Guilt rose up like bile in his throat. "None of this explains why you thought I would hurt her like that."

"Don't blame Gaby. She had other things on her mind, and I never asked her about the situation with you. I was angry. I've always felt a sort of protectiveness toward Gaby. She's been friends with Heather for a long time. I suppose I view her as a little sister. I also felt guilty because Heather and I introduced the two of you. I was upset to hear you had paid her off."

"She didn't have a job at my insistence," he explained. "Our contract had a clause I wrote in for her protection. She got fifty thousand if we broke up after two years. I didn't miss the money. I signed over her car, too." He thought for a moment. "I didn't see it here. She was driving some compact."

"She sold the BMW to pay for her medical bills. She didn't have insurance, and that money you gave her didn't go far. She still owes a hundred thousand. She was going to forgo the reconstructive surgery because she couldn't afford a plastic surgeon. Again, Heather convinced her to let us cover it. She still tries to pay me back."

Cal was still pissed at Heather, but it also seemed like he owed her. "How much was it? I'll write you a check."

"Don't worry about it. I took care of it. She won't let me pay the rest of her bills, but she did let me give her a job. She's managing the island." He said the last bit with the slightest wince.

Cal went still again. "My Gabrielle is managing your sex resort?"

Greg flashed a short grin. "She's really good at it. You would be surprised how hard it is to keep a good manager out there. Don't get pissed at me. She needed it. It took her away from everything."

"Yes, everything like hospitals and medical personnel to monitor her condition," Cal complained. It hadn't even been a year since her surgery. What had he read? A cancer patient couldn't consider herself safe until she was in remission for five years. Gabrielle needed checkups and doctors and the best care money could provide. "Did you think about that for a minute?"

Greg sat back, watching him. "Her second in command is a registered nurse. I hired him myself. She isn't a fragile flower, Cal. She's strong and smart. She has had all her checkups. That's what she's in town for. Heather took her today, and the doctors are very happy with her progress. Look, I am really sorry about this. I acted like an ass. I distanced when I should have had it out with you, but I let Heather and Gaby convince me to let it be."

"I didn't help by pulling back. I haven't called you or talked about anything but business. If I had just fucking called you, maybe I could have been there for her." It was his own stubborn fault. After Gabrielle had left, he'd closed down. Now that he looked back, it was like she had walked out of his life, taking with her everything that made it worth living.

"You can stop worrying about her. Actually, I'm glad to find out you still care about her. Maybe you can talk to her. I'd like to introduce her to some Doms I know. It's been long enough. She won't be happy in a vanilla relationship, but she's very shy. She's worried about her body. I tried introducing her to Harrison tonight, though according to Heather she seemed to have a better connection with the head of security. Crazy thing is, he's apparently in the lifestyle. She's still interested in a Dominant partner. I don't know that he's the one I would pair her with. It would go better if you could convince her it's all right for her to join us at the club. She can mix and mingle."

The very thought made his blood pressure rise. "Why the fuck would I want my sub mingling with a bunch of horny Doms?"

A knowing smile played on Greg's mouth. "What are you saying?"

"I'm saying stop trying to set up my sub with another Dom." Cal ground the words out. He knew he sounded crazy, but it didn't matter. He wasn't sure what he was feeling. All he knew was that things weren't finished between him and Gabrielle.

Chapter Two

Two weeks later, Gaby let the sun warm her face, and a strange sort of contentment suffused her. It wasn't happiness exactly. It was calm. She was calm here. It had happened the minute she got off the plane. A sense of peace passed over her like a warm wave.

Some people called it island time. The world seemed to slow down on a tropical island, and the little things didn't seem so insurmountable. With the sun warm on her face and the sound of the ocean in her ears, she seemed far from that place where her heart had been broken. This was a different world, and she had another chance here.

She wiggled her toes in the thick Caribbean sand and smiled at the couple walking past.

"Gaby, isn't it a lovely day?" A gorgeous redhead in a teeny tiny white bikini called out a greeting. The woman held hands with a man she had not come to the resort with. Gaby was pretty sure her husband was fucking a blonde in the hot tub. She had briefly glimpsed the couple as she'd instructed the staff to clean the deck. The couple hadn't even looked up from what they were doing.

Oh, the joys of swingers weekend.

But then it also reminded her exactly how far she'd come. A year ago she'd been her Master's kept plaything, coddled and hidden away from the world's dirty secrets. Well, the ones that weren't Cal's dirty secrets. Now she was the chick who dealt with the secrets, who kept everything running smoothly so those secrets never had to come out into the open.

When she thought about it, she was kind of a badass.

"It certainly is lovely." She nodded and gave the guests a friendly wave. The temporary couple walked off looking for privacy. It surprised her, since most of the couples didn't bother with anything as bourgeois as privacy. Sometimes she wondered where Greg had found his first manager. She was the second to manage this little piece of paradise, but she had no illusions that running a fetish resort required a certain sense of humor many people didn't have.

"Seriously? Half an hour ago I saw that guy with two brunettes and a totally hot hockey player," a familiar voice said.

Gaby turned and gave the newcomer her most brilliant smile. He shook his head as he watched the couple walk down the beach.

"We're supposed to pretend we don't recognize the famous people," she reminded her dear friend Cody. He leaned into her. Cody didn't believe in personal space when it came to his friends. Gaby slipped her arms through his. She loved how tactile he was. She could always count on a hug from him. "Especially when they swing both ways."

A decadent grin crossed Cody's face. He was a metro hottie with stylish dark hair and green eyes. He used far more product on his hair than she used on hers. When it came to style, she could learn a lot from him. "Honey, he was swinging more than two ways. I'd love to see what that man could do with a hockey stick and a tube of lube."

Gaby laughed and pushed affectionately at him. "Pervert."

"I wouldn't work here if I wasn't, G." His green eyes had that sparkle in them that told Gaby someone hot was on the horizon. "Speaking of perverts…the man in the Angelina Suite is so hot, I think I could die."

A smile slid across her face. She checked her watch. It was an hour before she had to check in on the luncheon arrangements. Her staff was a well-oiled machine. It made her life fairly easy and gave her time to listen to Cody's amazingly detailed physical descriptions of hot guys. She sank down into the sand and patted the ground next to her. "Hit me."

Cody sighed as he joined her. "Okay, where to begin? Naturally, he's gorgeous. He's roughly six-two."

"Linebacker or swimmer?" Hot guys came in two categories in Cody's world.

"Oh, swimmer. He's lean, but incredibly strong. Big broad shoulders, but not overly muscled. He works out, but it's not his whole life. His hair is dark as midnight. His face isn't perfect. He's hit thirty-five the hard way, but life and experience are written all over him."

Gaby snorted. "You should really be writing romance novels."

He waved her off. "His eyes are blue. They're a deep blue, and when he smiles, which he rarely does, there are these great creases around them. They give him character. He has sensual lips. No man should have those lips. I can feel them wrapped around my cock right now."

"Don't tell me he's gay," she protested playfully. Everyone was gay in Cody's fantasies. Even the most macho of men secretly harbored a love for guys in Cody's world. "You just ruined all my daydreams."

Cody looked serious for a moment, his brows coming together as he thought. "He's not gay. I'm out of luck there, but he's also not looking for a quick hookup. I showed him around a little. He wasn't interested in the amenities and he definitely wasn't looking at any of the hot bodies around us. I'm not sure why he's here this weekend. You know I've been around the lifestyle for a very, very long time."

Cody's parents were a D/s pair. They'd been in a loving relationship for thirty years. Cody often claimed his parents' comfort with themselves had led to his own pain-free acceptance of his sexuality.

"This guy isn't a swinger, and he's straight as an arrow, unfortunately," Cody said with a rueful sigh. "He's a Dom. Trust me, I know one when I see one."

"Did Heather send him?" She bit back a groan. She wouldn't put it past her longtime friend to send her a blind date. "She's been on my ass to find another Dom. I can't seem to get her and Greg to understand that I don't want another one."

Cody's eyebrow shot straight up. "You want a vanilla boy?"

She shrugged. "Sure, why not? Maybe I want a plain, old, boring love affair where I don't have to kneel at his feet and call him Sir.

Maybe I don't want to get tied up or have my ass spanked the second I step out of line. Maybe I don't want to get tortured by someone who makes me come for hours and then gently bathes me."

Cody coughed. It sounded suspiciously like "bullshit."

"I'm serious. I want a regular relationship this time," she said firmly. The truth was she wasn't sure what she wanted. She knew it was far too soon to get seriously involved with another Dom. Maybe one day. Years from now. Decades. "But a hot affair for a weekend is a completely different story."

"Now you're talking. I think sex would make you feel good. I think righteously nasty sex will make you feel even better." His handsome face was deceptively innocent. He touched his hand to his heart. "You should listen to me. I'm your murse."

Gaby rolled her eyes but leaned into him all the same. He called himself a murse, a meshing of male and nurse.

Cody Linwood was the best present Heather and Greg could have given her. He was the registered nurse who had helped her through her surgery. Cody had been the one to push and prod her into getting better. He'd been the one to hold her hand when she came out of surgery in so much pain she thought she would die. He'd heard her crying for Callum.

She shook off the thought as she brushed the sand from her khaki shorts. Being the manager of Decadence Resort didn't call for formal clothes. Her staff had simple uniforms, but she tended to wear whatever she liked.

"You said he was in the Angelina Suite? Maybe I'll take him a gift basket." She shook her head when she saw the excited look in Cody's eyes. "Don't think it's going anywhere. He's still a guest. I just want to take a look. If he's as hot as you say he is, maybe I'll make an exception."

Maybe she would. It was time to put distance between herself and Callum. She had to get over him or it would ruin what should be a good part of her life. She was young. She was freaking healthy.

It was time to embrace everything life had to offer.

"I stand ready to take over so you can debauch yourself for the weekend." He gave her a saucy salute.

She had to smile as she walked up toward the gorgeous

plantation-style resort she called home. She wouldn't actually start a red-hot affair with the Dom in the Angelina Suite. Probably not. Maybe not.

But it couldn't hurt to look.

* * * *

Twenty minutes later, Gaby checked herself out in the ornate mirror outside the resort's most expensive suite. She needed to talk to reservations and the front desk. They should have notified her when the suite was reserved. She hadn't checked on his name, but she knew he had to be a VIP if he could afford the Angelina Suite.

But she could deal with the breakdown in protocols later. For now, it was time to be the gracious host and figure out if this Dom was here to play or here at Heather's behest.

She took a hard look at herself. Her brown hair was starting to get long enough to curl. In this case her island worked against her. The tropical humidity was frizzing her out. She tried to smooth it down. It was too hot to wear much makeup, other than a bit of mascara and some lip-gloss. At least her boobs looked good. They were perky in her neat little polo. And despite what her asshole former Master had said, she was gaining back the weight she'd lost. Her curves were coming back with a vengeance. If she didn't stay away from the buffet, she would be right back at pleasingly plump.

She held the very nice fruit basket in one hand and plastered a professional smile on her face as she knocked on the door to the suite.

"Come on in," a masculine voice said. The door swung open, but all she saw was a nice view of a ripped back as the man turned away. "I'll slip into some pants and be right with you."

The gorgeous towel-clad figure with the deep voice disappeared behind the bathroom door without ever letting her see his face.

He reminded her of Callum. Yeah, probably everyone would right now. And there went the slight possibility of a hot affair. She sighed as she looked around the suite. Everything appeared to be in its proper place. It was a gorgeously decorated room. The art on the walls were abstracts done by up-and-coming artists. The sofa and chairs were all Italian leather, and her feet sank into the rich carpet that covered the floor.

She opened the curtains to give the new guest the best view of the ocean. The Angelina Suite had a large balcony that overlooked the blue Caribbean. There was no way she could ignore the impulse to walk out there. While her guest was getting ready, she opened the glass door and stepped out. That was perfection right there. White sand beaches and a turquoise blue ocean. The sun sparkled on the waves as they lazily took and gave up territory.

Yes, this was where she needed to be.

Couples walked hand in hand. A woman played like a child in the sand, building castles that would last only as long as the low tide. This was a place to play, to explore, to leave the real world behind. She took a deep breath. The day smelled like clean ocean breeze and sandalwood. The smell brought her right back to Cal. When he'd put his arms around her, she had been able to smell the soap he used, clean sandalwood. The scent had always made her feel safe.

God, was she ever going to forget him?

It had been two weeks since that scene in the gazebo and every single night since she'd dreamed about him. Good dreams. Shitty dreams. It didn't matter. He was the focus of them all.

The first week had been fueled by a righteous fury. She'd come back to the island with all manner of revenge in her head. She could fuck him over in several ways. But gradually, her rage had fizzled down to a sadness she couldn't seem to shake. Revenge wouldn't fix things and it wasn't her way. By the second week, she'd smiled and went about her business, but ripping Callum out of her heart had been hard. The truth was she felt a little empty now.

She wasn't ready for this.

What was she doing here? She was never going to hit on this guy, no matter how hot he was. She needed time. She needed to be with herself for a while, maybe a long while.

She stepped back in the room and made her way to the front door.

"Uhm, I just wanted to drop off your gift basket and welcome you to the resort. If you need anything, please call the lobby." She had her hand on the door when a voice stopped her.

"Why don't I simply call you, Gabrielle?" The voice was dark and deep. It was a voice that haunted her.

45

Her breath caught and she forced herself to turn. "Callum?"

He was a sight in black jeans and nothing else. His dark hair had been towel dried and curled around his ears. A sheen of moisture gleamed across his cut torso. Her mouth watered at the sight of his six-pack. There was no need to see his muscular legs or anything else the jeans hid. That amazing masculine body of his was burned into her memory.

"In the flesh, so to speak." There was a satisfied smile on his face that told her he was reading her like a book. He'd always known the effect he had on her. "It's good to see you. I was worried I would get here and you would somehow be gone again. God, I didn't like the way we parted and I thought we should talk."

"There's nothing to talk about." She should have expected this, though she'd rather thought he would call and not show up in person. He hadn't known about the cancer. He felt bad. Therefore he was here to assuage his conscience. There was absolutely nothing for him to feel guilty about. She forced herself to smile. "I get it. You feel bad. You didn't know when you pulled that complete dick move in the gazebo. I understand and you're forgiven. Now, I have work to do. Please let the front desk know if you need anything. I hope you enjoy your stay."

She turned to go.

"Gabrielle." He barked her name like an order.

Gaby stopped, unconsciously used to following his commands. She stared at the door, unable to push through it. Why did this man have such power over her? Why did it have to be him?

"You will not walk away from me," he said in that deep chocolate voice of his. Somehow, even when he was angry as hell, that voice was sex and sin to her. "We *are* going to talk this out. You lied to me. You left me under false pretenses. I want some answers."

Was he serious? She turned, facing him. "I don't owe you anything, Cal. I honored our contract and I left when I felt the relationship was done. If you're pissed about the money you gave me, I'll find a way to pay you back."

His fists clenched at his sides, a sure sign he was emotional. It almost never came across in his voice, but she could tell by the tension of his body. "I don't give a shit about the money. I want to know why you didn't tell me you had cancer."

It was the one word that could make her beyond tired. Just saying the word made her weary. It wouldn't do any good to reopen old wounds. "It doesn't matter now. I'm fine. You're fine. We were in a relationship that was going nowhere. Now we can both find better partners."

His eyes latched on hers, real heat coming through them. "Is that why you're here? Are you fucking the guests to figure out what you need?"

Hot anger rushed through her, making her forget her previous weariness. He had no right to question her. No rights to her at all. "Screw you, Callum. Like I said, call the desk if you need anything."

He reached out to grab her. His hand was gentle but insistent. "Gabrielle, wait. I'm sorry. I'm screwing it up again. You know I'm not good at this. Please. I only want to talk. I'll keep a civil tongue in my head. Please have dinner with me. I've spent the last two weeks working day and night so I could spend time with you. Check through my things. I didn't even bring my cell."

Her eyes widened. Cal was surgically attached to his cell phone. He was always working. His hands moved gently, stroking up and down her arms. It was a familiar gesture. She knew she should pull away, but she found herself unwilling to leave him. "Are you serious?"

"I shut down my office and cleared my cases," he explained. "You were wrong. You said we were fine, but I'm not fine. I haven't been since you walked out on me."

She was quiet for a moment. It was hard to believe he'd shut his office down. Even for a few days. Whatever he had to say to her must be damn serious. It seemed beyond dangerous to spend time with him. Any weakness would be used ruthlessly. It wasn't cruelty on his part. It was merely who he was.

She should walk away.

"All right." The words came out before she could think to stop them. And her voice came out softer than she liked. She'd replied to him like the old Gabrielle, like the submissive replying to her Master. She squared her shoulders and looked him right in the eyes, forcing herself to speak in a strong tone. "But just dinner. Nothing else."

He smiled, showing even, white teeth. He held his hands up in supplication. "Just dinner. Just talking. I have questions I need you to answer. In return, I'll answer any questions you have for me."

She swallowed. Was he serious? When they had been together, he'd blocked off huge portions of his life that she wasn't allowed to discuss with him. She should still walk away, but she was curious. "Any questions?"

He nodded slowly. "Any. Does that tell you how desperate I am? I need this. I need to understand what went wrong."

Of all the reasons he was here, that one made her soften. Perhaps they both needed some closure. "I eat at seven in the main dining room."

"Gabrielle?" He said her name like a prayer. It forced her to turn and truly look at him. She noticed the weariness around his eyes and the way his forehead creased with worry. "Thank you."

She nodded and walked out of the room, her heart thudding in her chest.

* * * *

Callum watched her across the table, hating the fact that she'd chosen the chair across from him. Before, she would have settled in next to him. Even when they were in a booth, he preferred her beside him, their bodies brushing up against each other. The way she was sitting was merely more proof that they were broken.

Not broken up. It was worse than that. They were broken and he had to see if there was any way to put them back together again.

He glanced around the main dining room as she studied the menu. He was fairly certain she had that sucker memorized, but tonight was about making her comfortable. If she wasn't ready to talk, he would give her a couple of minutes. In the meantime, he would look around and get a feel for this place where she worked.

The dining room was a vision of modern elegance. The colors were muted, with bold swipes of color planted around. The filmy curtains were a stunning peacock blue. The tables were covered in clean white linens. It was very different from the old, sturdy hotel Greg had sent him out to scout a few years ago. This island resort had been one of the first deals he'd brokered for Greg. At the time, the place had been lovely but dated.

Even Cassie had noted the hotel's old-fashioned feel on the many occasions he had taken her here before she'd died.

How much had Gabrielle contributed to the stunning rehab of the place? He saw touches of her aesthetic everywhere. She had exquisite taste. She had taken their home to an entirely different level.

Why had he never brought her here?

The waiter stepped up and smiled at Gabrielle with obvious affection. Cal had noticed that her staff seemed to adore her. That didn't surprise him. His office staff had gone into mourning after she'd left him.

He couldn't take his damn eyes off her.

Greg had said she was strong, but she looked fragile to him. She was lovely in a purple skirt and low-cut white blouse. The white of the blouse contrasted with her tan skin. Still, she was too thin. Was she eating properly? Working too much? How was stress going to affect her recovery? This was a stressful job.

He wanted nothing more than to take her into his arms and let her know that he would handle everything from here on out. He would talk to her doctors. He'd already dealt with the bill collectors, but he didn't mention they wouldn't bother her again. If this worked, all she would have to do was rest and concentrate on being in remission. He would take care of her.

The way he should have the first time around.

"Are you ready to order your entrees?" the waiter asked.

They ordered and then were left sitting and staring at one another.

He had to make this easy on her. He couldn't simply jump right on the topic. "So what's the toughest thing about running this place?"

He would show her how interested he was in her work. Then he would gently try to take her away from her work. Yeah, that was the smart play.

"You wouldn't believe how hard it is to keep a cleaning staff," she explained with mirth in her eyes. She was so animated. Her eyes lit up when she talked about working at the resort. "They all come in and are excited about working at someplace this beautiful, but the first orgy they have to clean up after makes them think twice. Can you believe that Greg actually ordered cloth couches? They're gorgeous, but do you know how hard those suckers are to clean? I switched everything to leather. It's much simpler. He moaned about the cost, but then he saw how fast our cleaning bill went down."

Her expression was so cute he had to laugh. Then he thought about the fact that she ran orgies and he frowned.

"What's wrong, Cal? Don't like the thought of your former sub organizing the orgy? That's a terrible word for it. There is truly no organization to it. But I am the woman who makes sure the room is reserved and fully stocked with the two things every good orgy needs."

"Dare I ask?"

"Condoms and Gatorade. Lots of electrolytes get lost in all that exercise," she explained. "Sometimes I feel like a coach, you know. I load 'em up with fluids and send them right back on the field."

He rather thought she was teasing him, like he was being a prissy ass. "I'm sorry. I suppose this is one of those things I likely won't get over. Sex has always been too intimate to share with a group."

Her eyes widened and he was surprised to find she had a "dumbass said what" face.

"I didn't say I had a problem with public sex. I've got many exhibitionist tendencies. I have a problem having sex *with* the public. And yes, it bothers me that you would be on the sidelines during something like that. What if someone thought you were up for grabs?"

"I have security. And I'm not really in there," she admitted. "I was teasing you. We have some monitors but I sit that one out."

The waiter set their salads in front of them and walked away, hiding a smile behind his hand.

He leaned in, unable to hold back. "Are you sure this is the best place for you? Shouldn't you be close to a hospital?"

They had tiptoed around the subject of her illness. She had acknowledged that she had cancer, but now it was in remission. It seemed to be all she was willing to say on the subject.

"I love the sun and beach," she replied with a dreamy smile. "And Cody is a murse, so we're good."

"Murse?"

She speared a cucumber. "It's his name for male nurse. Apparently, it's a very hot job for a gay man. He claims to get a lot of tail out of it. Anyway, he also rides my ass about my eating habits and checks me on an altogether too often basis. He deeply enjoys taking my blood pressure."

She popped the little vegetable in her mouth, her lips caressing it briefly before it disappeared.

Callum played with his fork. He wanted to reach out and grab her hand. He used to like to play with her fingers while they ate. Even better than that, when they were alone, he loved to pull her into his lap and feed her. During those times she was naked, of course. She was almost always naked for him. He took a quick swallow of his tea. The thought of pulling her close was giving him an erection. "I'm glad Greg hired him."

"He wouldn't give me the job unless Cody came along," Gaby admitted.

They were silent for a moment, each halfheartedly eating the lovely salads in front of them. When had it gotten hard to talk to her? It used to be easy.

"Why didn't you tell me?" He carefully kept all accusation out of his voice.

Gaby's gorgeous gray-green eyes suddenly found the white table linen endlessly fascinating. He noticed the fine lines on her face that hadn't been there before. He wanted to lean over and kiss them, enjoying the lovely way her face was maturing. Somehow those lines didn't take away from her beauty. They simply added texture and contour to the work of art that was her face. She would be beautiful at eighty.

He would still want her. He would never stop wanting her.

He reached out and forced her chin gently up. He looked into her eyes. "It might not have been the best relationship of your life, but I was honest with you. And I tried to take care of you."

She nodded, her eyes wide. "It wasn't your fault that you couldn't love me."

Every word out of her mouth made him feel guilty. "Did you think I would kick you out? That's what's haunting me—the idea that you thought I would be that cruel. How could you believe that?"

51

"I didn't," she replied. "I knew you would stand by me."

He was terribly confused. "Then why did you leave?"

She was quiet for a moment, as though trying to figure out exactly what to say to him. "I got the news and it hit me hard. I tried to think of a way I could tell you and I kept coming back to the fact that you had already been through this once. I left because I knew how hard it was on you when Cassie died. I made the decision to not put you through that again. I was going to leave no matter what you said. If you had magically changed your mind and told me you loved me, I still would have left. I guess I needed to hear the words. I knew what you would say. I had to hear it from you so I could move on with my life."

Of all the things he'd expected to hear, this hadn't been one of them. He'd expected her to cry and tell him how she'd been scared he would reject her. Or that he would be angry and cold. But to hear that no matter what he'd said, he hadn't had a chance? That she'd needed to trap him into saying something so she could move on? How could she have been thinking of moving on when all he'd been thinking about was her? "And it didn't matter that I cared about you? It didn't matter that I had built a life with you at the center?"

Her short brown hair shook as she sighed. "I was incidental to your life, Cal. I was something you collected, like your art."

"How can you say that?" The accusation didn't sit well with him. "I took care of you. I made sure you had everything you needed."

"And you canceled most of the plans we made," she said softly. There was no real heat behind her words. It seemed like something she had accepted a long time ago. "I remember our first anniversary. I planned an amazing meal. I made your favorite lasagna. I put on a French maid's outfit and waited. Do you recall what happened that night?"

He felt himself flush. Yes, he remembered. He'd gotten a line on a group of buildings Greg had been eyeing for years. He'd left the office without even heading home. "I called you from the airport on my way to New York."

"And my birthday?"

"I'm sure I forgot that altogether."

She pushed her salad around on her plate, and he wished he'd never asked the original question. She'd been so happy talking about her work. "Your admin remembered. I should have known it was her. She sent me roses."

He would never have bought her roses. "You hate roses. You like lilies."

"I do," she replied. "I guess your admin didn't have a list of my favorite things."

Now he did what came naturally. He reached out and took her hand. It was time to open up to her. He'd hated the last ten months with a passion. He was more than willing to apologize if it bought him a second's goodwill with her. Despite his earlier promise, he wanted to end the evening buried deep inside her body.

"I am sorry about that, Gabrielle. Maybe I did pay too much attention to work, but you were always in my thoughts. I got flustered at that meeting in New York because I missed you. Sometimes I had to force myself to focus because if I didn't, I would have called you just to say hello or to find out what you were doing and what you were wearing. If you look back at our relationship, you'll remember that I actually did that often. I called you when I was away simply to hear your voice. Oh, I made up excuses. I gave you lists of things to do, but mostly I wanted to know you were there. And I wanted to pretend you were naked."

"I'm sure I was wearing very little at the time," she said with a wistful smile.

He squeezed her hand, a bit afraid to let it go. "I know I didn't show it, but you were the center of my world. You weren't a convenience for me. I thought I was building a life for us."

"But you didn't want to marry me or have children with me." Her eyes were soft as she shook her head. "There wasn't a future in that for me."

He felt his mouth firm in frustration. He felt trapped, though, strangely, not by her. That night when she'd made her ultimatum, he'd been wrong to blame her. This was a trap of his own making. Despite what she'd said, he knew damn well if he'd handled her better, she would have been in his bed the next morning and inevitably she would have turned to him and told him everything. He'd reacted poorly. He wasn't going to make the same mistake.

53

"Does it have to be mapped out? Why couldn't we just be happy? Why do we have to bring a bunch of kids into the equation?"

The very thought of children made his throat close up. Children were fragile. Children were small and vulnerable. Women still died giving birth. He couldn't handle that, not if he had the choice.

She pulled her hand out of his. Her posture became rigid, and he missed her previous comfort. "We don't have to do anything, Cal. We aren't together anymore. You don't have to worry about me having your unwanted babies."

His fist hit the table. "Damn it. I didn't say that. I certainly didn't mean anything like that. You never once mentioned that you wanted kids before the night you left me. Not once. I thought we were on the same page. Can you let me catch up?"

"Will you?" She seemed more curious than truly interested in his answer to the question.

"I don't know," he muttered, irritated at the way the conversation had gone.

"It's okay." Her hands came out to cover his. She'd always been quick to comfort him. "Forget I said anything. How long are you here?"

"A week." He loved the way her hands felt against his. He had one week to try to win her back.

"Can we shelve the relationship stuff? Look, I've spent a lot of time thinking about us. I'm not sure we were ever going to work. It's as much my fault as yours. I pretended to be something I'm not. I'm not as submissive as I played at. I like it for sex, but it was annoying outside the bedroom. I'm more independent now. I went through something that made me understand how strong I am. I'm not a slave anymore."

"I never thought of you that way."

She took a deep breath. "But a slave is what you seem to need. I should never have gotten involved with you. I wasn't what you needed."

How could she possibly think that? She had been everything he needed. He'd been as happy as he could have imagined himself being for the years they were together. At first, it had been about sex, but after about six months, he'd gotten comfortable and settled into the relationship. It had been the single best relationship of his life. He'd come to rely on it, on her.

She'd given him everything he could have wanted.

"You were exactly what I needed," he admitted, a hole opening up inside him. "I wasn't what you needed."

She'd been right that night months ago. She'd played the role of his wife to perfection. She'd kept his house, hosted his parties and dinners, and kept the books. He'd never had to worry about anything beyond work. Between Gaby and his longtime assistant, Helen, he'd been covered on every front. Now, he wondered how hard it had been on her to think of herself essentially as an employee rather than a beloved female.

Her mouth curled up in the semblance of a smile. "I thought I needed you. It's funny now. I was twenty-six and so sure that I knew what I was doing. I was sure that all you needed was time. I met you and I knew you were the one for me. It was like a lightning bolt."

He remembered the night like it was yesterday. Greg had introduced them. He'd heard about Heather's close friend for months, but he hadn't cared. He hadn't been interested in a relationship. Cassie had only been gone for a year when he'd met Gabrielle. It had been far too soon to think about anything beyond his physical needs. Annoyance had been his major emotion that night. He didn't want to be polite to one of Heather's friends.

All of that had changed the minute he looked at her. She'd smiled shyly at him, and he was lost.

"I knew you didn't want anything serious…"

He cut her off. He wasn't going to allow her to rewrite their history. "I signed a contract with you two weeks after we met. I know I wasn't interested in marriage, but that contract was serious to me."

She took a sip of her drink and nodded, obviously conceding the point. "All right. I'll rephrase. I knew you weren't interested in anything beyond a D/s relationship."

He hated the way she put that but forced himself to remain silent. He wasn't going to win her over by arguing semantics.

"So I became your perfect sub," she explained. "I'd never been in a twenty-four seven relationship before. I never even wanted one, but I knew it was the only way to keep you, so I tried it. When I think about it, I was really arrogant. Stupid and way younger than I am now. I thought if I became exactly what you wanted, you would love me. I thought after a while you would realize how perfect we were together and we'd be married and have some kids and everything would be hearts and flowers and happily ever after."

"I never promised you that." He'd promised her the exact opposite.

"I know. It's all right, Cal. I'm trying to explain. It wasn't your fault. It was mine. I knew what you wanted, and I tried to change you anyway. It's a mistake I've heard a lot of women make. You told me you would never love another woman, and I arrogantly thought I could change your mind." She sat back in her chair, her shoulders straight, her head held high. "I was wrong to do that to you. I knew from the moment I met you that I wanted to marry you and have babies with you. I should have honored your feelings and walked away that night."

He swallowed a long drink of Scotch, his hand clutching the glass like it was some kind of life raft. He wouldn't have let her walk away. He'd known he had to have her.

"Instead, I forced us both to waste three years of our lives," she continued. "So, I want you to know that I don't hate you. I'm pissed at myself, but I certainly don't hate you. You couldn't help the fact that I wasn't someone you could love. I know you feel bad because you didn't know about the cancer."

"You didn't tell me." He growled the accusation.

"Hey," she said softly. It was the voice she used to soothe him. "I didn't want to worry you. It wasn't your problem. It was mine. I knew it would bring back all kinds of bad memories. You didn't need to go through losing someone again and I wasn't sure I would make it."

His hands clenched. He wanted her to hold his hands again. "That wasn't your call to make. You should have told me. You should have told me the minute you suspected something was wrong. I would have taken care of it. I would have taken care of you. I consider it tantamount to lying that you kept this from me."

She shrugged. The negligent gesture enraged him. It took everything he had not to toss her over his shoulder and find someplace more private. "I wasn't anything more than a nice body in

56

bed with you, Cal. You wouldn't have thought my body was so nice after chemo decimated me. And you were right. You don't like silicone. You wouldn't want me now. I saved myself some heartache. I have no doubt you would have done your duty by me. But that was all it would have been."

"Goddamn it, Gabrielle," he practically shouted. He slapped at the table, making everything on it jump. "Give me some fucking credit."

He flushed as he realized he'd lost his temper in front of a roomful of guests. Curious eyes were all around him. Naturally his anger was utterly wasted on Gabrielle. She rolled her eyes his way and sighed. It made his hands shake with the need to turn her little rear over his knee and reintroduce her to the boss. His sub needed a spanking.

"Calm down, Cal," she said in an even voice that set his temper on edge.

He leaned forward. "I am trying to be fair with you. I'm trying to have a conversation about this rather than giving you a lecture."

"How very kind of you." There was a quirky smile on her face.

Her perky ass wasn't all he'd smack. He'd spank her pussy, too. He'd slap at it until she begged him to let her come. By the time he was through punishing her, she wouldn't be thinking of anything having to do with her illness or her insecurities. All that would be left was the driving need to orgasm. She might not understand it, but she needed their relationship more than ever. "Don't push me, pet. I won't hesitate to redden your rear in front of these people. They won't help you."

She frowned, but at least he got a blush out of her. "I'm not yours to discipline anymore."

The last bit was said with no small amount of hesitance. It was still in her nature to obey him, to want his dominance. He still had a shot. He stared at her, trying to let her feel his hunger. He wanted her to sense the predator he kept carefully hidden behind designer suits. Maybe she hadn't really known him. He'd never been forced to pursue her, so she'd never been treated to the beast he knew lived buried inside him.

"That is not your decision to make. You can take the collar off,

57

but I'll put it right back on now that I understand why you left. I fully intend to have that collar around your neck by the time I leave here. You'll be on the plane beside me."

She turned the slightest bit white as her fingers tightened around the fork in her hand. "I get that you're angry. I did something that prevented you from performing the duties you feel you owed me. I understand you want to punish me."

He made sure his eyes were very serious as he interrupted her. "This isn't about punishing you, Gabrielle. This is about making things right. We should never have split up. I was wrong to allow you to leave. You left under a misconception. I intend to correct it."

Her mouth tightened. "Do you have any idea how arrogant you sound? Allow me to leave? I wasn't under a misconception. We had a difference of opinion. I wanted to get married, and you didn't."

His heart pounded, but he forced his face to remain relaxed. He'd known this was what he needed to do, and he was going to get through it. He'd made a terrible mistake ten months back. She could argue all she liked that she would have left no matter what, but he knew differently. He'd spent the last two weeks thinking about what he owed his submissive. Once he'd decided what he owed Gabrielle, he'd known his path was chosen. No matter what promises he'd made in the past. He had an obligation to her in the here and now. "I've changed my mind. We'll stop in Vegas on our way home."

Chapter Three

Gaby felt her mouth drop open. "Why would we stop in Vegas?"

It was a stupid question and she knew it. Cal knew it, too. The smug smile on his face told her so.

"We'll stop there so we can get married. You said you would be happy if we got married. I've thought about this long and hard and decided that it's a reasonable request."

The dinner was not going as she planned. She had thought she could sit and logically work through the end of their relationship with Callum. It would be like a therapy session they both needed. She owed him an explanation. She expected him to yell at her. She expected him to try to get her in bed. She didn't expect a marriage proposal.

Although it hadn't been much of a proposal. "I'm not marrying you."

One elegant eyebrow arched up. "And why not? You said this is what you wanted."

"No, I wanted you to fall in love with me. I wanted you to want to marry me," she ground out. It should be plain. She shouldn't have to humiliate herself to make him understand.

His deep blue eyes narrowed and she felt the weight of his intensity. "You told me what you needed, and I'm giving it to you. I have a ring in my bag. If it's not nice enough for you, I'll pick another one, but I assure you the diamond is of the highest quality."

"I don't care about the diamond." Her temper was a live flame in her body, stoked by every word he said. She'd dreamed of this moment, had fantasy after fantasy about how he would propose once he realized they were perfect together. Never, in all those daydreams, had he proposed to her because she "needed" it. Tears threatened and she was angry with herself because a part of her still wanted to take this gesture of his and run with it. That part of her that would never stop loving him told her to put that ring on her finger and his love would come later. It was an illusion, a little girl fantasy she had to let go of.

"I should think you would care about your engagement ring," he replied. "I spent an enormous amount of time making sure it was the best I could buy for you. I designed the mounting myself."

"I'm sure it's lovely." It was past time to end this discussion. She stood up suddenly. He wasn't going to be reasonable. She had no idea what his game was, but she wasn't going to play. "It doesn't matter because I have no intention of marrying a man who doesn't love me."

He remained seated. "Do you want me to say the words? I can certainly say the words if you need them."

He looked cool and collected in his white dress shirt and neatly pressed slacks. Only Callum could keep his clothes perfect in the tropics. Everyone else wore shorts or casual dresses, and even those got wrinkled in the heat, but Cal looked like he'd walked straight off the pages of a magazine. Her hair wilted in the heat. It bothered her that Callum's hair curling merely made him more appealing.

Tears were threatening, and she'd promised herself she wouldn't cry over him again. What she wouldn't give for him to say he loved her if he really meant it. "It doesn't mean anything if you don't feel it. We both know you don't love me."

He stared at her for a moment, his eyes tired as he ran a hand through his thick hair. "Do we? I know I've missed you. I know I would greatly prefer to have you in my life. Why can't that be a version of love?"

"Because it isn't." There was no talking to him. He'd decided he wanted her back and he would be relentless. If she wasn't careful she would end up right back where she'd started—his plaything, useful but ultimately empty and replaceable. "I have some things I need to see to. I hope you enjoy the rest of your dinner."

His hand reached out to grab her arm. His face was a slab of granite. "I won't enjoy the evening without you, Gabrielle. I thought I made that clear. Don't walk away from me. I'm willing to sit and discuss this with you, but if you walk away, I'll be forced to try something else."

She stopped, well aware they were in the middle of the dining room and everyone could see them. "This isn't fair."

"It wasn't fair of you to walk out on me under false pretenses," he said in an altogether too reasonable voice. "Put the shoe on the other foot. How would you feel if I had been the one who walked away? If I hid a serious, potentially life-threatening illness from you, how would you feel? You could have died. Would I have even been informed? Would you have let me go on not knowing what had happened to you?"

He said it evenly, but she knew him. She could hear the emotion in his voice. It made her heart hurt because there was that kernel of true feeling she'd always known he had. It was an ember she'd never been able to stoke into a fire. "I figured Greg would tell you."

He laughed bitterly. "Of course. I'm sure he would have told me gently since you didn't bother to mention to him that I hadn't kicked you to the curb the minute I heard you were diagnosed with cancer."

"I didn't mean for that to happen." Gaby snatched her arm away. She backed up before he could get a hand on her again. "I'm sorry. I never said any such thing to him or anyone else. After I left you, I never talked about you to any of our friends. Not once. I need to go. I hope you enjoy your stay with us, Mr. Reed."

He cursed, but he didn't stand up to follow her. At least she didn't have to worry about that drama playing out in front of the dining room. She crossed the floor toward the exit as quickly as her heels would take her, feeling his eyes on her the whole time. A shiver raced along her skin and she was disconcerted to find it wasn't from fear. Oh, the fear was in there, but she couldn't fool herself. Being so close to Callum aroused her. She'd spent most of the last year worried that her sex drive was simply gone. Now she knew it had merely been waiting for the one man she shouldn't want.

She turned out of the dining room. Several staff members greeted her, but she simply nodded and kept walking, determined to put distance between herself and Cal. Outside. That was what she needed. She needed to feel the sand under her feet, to remind herself that she was here and different than before. This was her place of power, not his. Every instinct in her body wanted her to go back to Callum and sink to her knees. Cal would take care of her, but she didn't need that anymore. She was strong and powerful. She could handle everything on her own.

The minute she stepped outside, she felt like she could breathe again.

The moon was full, hanging low in the velvet sky as she slid out of her heels and let her toes wiggle in the still-warm sand. The Caribbean lay in front of her like a shimmering jewel. One deep breath and then another as she let the breeze soothe her heated skin. Cal had her stimulated on every level. Emotionally. Physically. There was no way to deny the effect he had on her. Being close to him set her every nerve on edge. It had been impossible not to reach out and touch him. She'd kept telling herself to keep her hands on the table, and yet they naturally sought out his skin.

A low moan broke through the quiet night. Ah, she was next to one of the hot tub areas. Everything at Decadence was built to accommodate sexual desire. It was a private club that served as a playground for the rich with exotic tastes. In accordance with its purpose, there were several "bathing" areas. One was ultramodern, with jets and bubbly hot water that covered what happened under it with its froth. One was attached to the pool, while another overlooked the ocean. This particular area was known as the Roman bath, and it was currently being put to the use Greg intended.

She glanced over, noting that there were five people in the bath area, two women and three men. The bath was a long, beautifully tiled tub surrounded by chaise lounges and palm trees. In this area all the food was finger food, grapes, and cheese, along with staff in togas to serve the guests. The men sat in the steaming tub watching as the women put on a show.

She should walk along the beach, get some perspective. She needed to think about what was going to happen when Cal showed up for round two, because there would definitely be another battle.

And yet she found herself standing there, watching. She'd been the manager here for almost a year and she never watched. Didn't have any interest, which was precisely why she was a good manager.

Now all she could think about was sex.

Two female bodies lay on top of a plush lounger, their limbs entwined. One blonde and a raven-haired beauty. The blonde was on her back with her legs spread as the dark-haired woman nestled her head at the juncture of her partner's thighs. The woman's tongue darted out to slide through her partner's pussy. The blonde spread her legs, showing off the wet juices that spilled onto her thighs.

She wasn't interested in women. She had nothing against them, but she'd always known she liked men. But there was something so erotic about the picture in front of her she couldn't deny it.

"Oh, yes." The blonde was moaning, her husky voice carried by the wind.

Gaby stood at the vine-covered fence separating the play area from the beach.

One of the men pulled himself up, perching on the side of the bath. He was muscular, with broad shoulders and neatly kept hair. He balanced on one arm, leaning back as his feet dangled in the steamy water. His big hand slid down his wet body. He cupped his heavy balls before traveling up to the thick base of his cock. He stroked himself up and down leisurely.

Gaby watched, remembering the silky skin that covered Callum's big cock. It was so beautiful. She loved the feel of him, the play of smooth and strong. Callum's cock was huge. The first time she'd seen it, her eyes had eaten it up. Her pussy had clenched at the thought of how well he'd fill her up. She loved how powerful she felt when he was in her hands. She would roll his balls against her palm and watch as his cock twitched, begging for attention. She would lick the head, paying special attention to the *V* on the underside. She would lick that spot over and over, teasing it before swallowing his dick whole.

Even though he barked orders at her, she was in control in those moments.

The man in front of her stroked himself, his cock pulsing. His eyes were locked on the women as they writhed in pleasure. The dark-haired woman licked and sucked at the blonde's clit.

The sight was an erotic jolt to Gaby's system. How long had it been since she had cupped her own mound and rode her fingers to pleasure? Frustrated tears filled her eyes. Sometimes it felt like her own body was a foreign thing she would never get used to again. It was a cruel twist of fate to Gaby's mind. She'd never been one of those women to question her sexuality. She'd been more than happy to take her pleasure. She hadn't had a ton of lovers, but she'd enjoyed almost all of them. The mistakes she'd made, she'd forgiven herself for. She'd accepted her submissive nature and dismissed anyone who looked down on her for it.

The loss of her sexual self was almost as devastating as the cancer itself.

The blonde cupped her full breasts as the black-haired woman pulled apart her labia, revealing the pink pearl hidden there. She sat up and looked down at her partner's clit, murmuring words Gaby couldn't quite hear. She could fill in the blanks. The dark-haired girl would tell the blonde how gorgeous her little clit was. She would tell her how it was sweet to taste that juicy pussy. The dark-haired woman's hand came out and slid across the clit in front of her before she leaned over to finish the job she'd started.

Her tongue darted out to tease the blonde's clit mercilessly. Gaby watched with breathless anticipation as a single finger was added. The blonde groaned and started to ride that finger, her hips pumping frantically. It wouldn't be enough. Not nearly. She knew that feeling, knew how desperate a woman could get when she was kept on the jagged edge. A woman on the edge would need way more than that little finger, but she would shove it in, trying to hit that sweet spot. Cal had done this to her so many times. He would tease her until she wanted to scream. She would try to move against him, try to force him to give her more.

That was when the discipline would begin.

No discipline for the blonde, however. Her partner simply smiled and gave her what she wanted. Two and then three fingers disappeared into the blonde's creamy pussy, and when the dark-haired woman leaned down and gave her clit a long, slow lick, the blonde's head began to thrash a little as she moaned.

Gaby glanced over at the men. The man sitting on the side was looking directly at her, and a slow smile spread across his face. He was a very attractive man with blond hair and Nordic blue eyes. His cock was long and thick. He brushed his thumb across the bulbous head. Even from her vantage, she could see the cream beginning to coat him, facilitating his masturbation. The muscles of his washboard abs rippled as he picked up the pace. He stared straight at Gaby as he pumped his cock harder and harder, pulling at it from base to head. His balls drew up tight and close to his body. His face flushed. Gaby could hear the blonde coming, but she couldn't take her eyes off the man. He breathed out and groaned as jets of cream began to coat his hands.

He winked at Gaby and mouthed, "Join me."

Gaby nearly jumped back. It was one thing to watch, another thing entirely to join in. She could imagine his horror when she got naked. He was practically perfect. How would he react to her breasts? How would he react to the freaky tattooed nipples she sported now? More than that, how could she even think about anyone else when Cal was here? That, above all else, made her want to run. She couldn't still be in love with Callum. A little panicked, Gaby took another step back and walked straight into a brick wall. Thick arms surrounded her.

"You have no idea how lucky you are you didn't take that asshole up on his invitation," Cal breathed darkly into her ear.

His arms wound around her waist. She was pierced by the sweet feeling it brought. She'd always felt safe in Callum's grip. Warmth flooded her system.

She remembered how he liked to sleep plastered against her. It had been difficult at first, but after a while, she came to crave the tangle of limbs Callum preferred to rest in. Even when he moved in his sleep, he pulled her along. She hadn't slept deeply in ten months. "I wasn't thinking about joining in."

"Good, because you would have been cleaning up a bloody mess, pet. I understand we have problems to iron out. Do not bring another man into them."

His hands moved up to cup her breasts. She tried to pull away.

"Stop it," he ordered in that deep voice that had her obeying almost mindlessly. She stilled in his arms. She could feel his rock-hard cock against her ass. "I'm not hurting you, Gabrielle. I promise my cock will stay in my pants. Relax. Let me make you feel good. Consider it payback for the blow job I stole."

She laughed at the thought. "You were never good at keeping it in your pants. I've heard endless stories of your conquests."

He stilled behind her. "That's not true." He turned her around and threaded his fingers through hers. He pulled her away from the bath area and down to the beach. It was quieter here, and he sank down into the sand, tugging her between his legs. "Gabrielle, I admit to having certain exotic tastes, but you're under a misconception about my level of experience."

His arms caged her, forcing her back against his chest. The cool breeze off the ocean caressed her skin. The moon was full and heavy in the sky. It was a truly romantic night. She felt surrounded by him, his arms almost a blanket around her skin. She should get up and leave, but she'd always been curious about Cal's past. The idea that she could learn what had been secret for so long kept her right where she was. "I was told you went through a sub a night before you met me."

He gently urged her head back as he spoke quietly. "I met you two weeks after the anniversary of my wife's death. Do you honestly believe I started fucking my way through the club when she was barely in the ground?"

He asked the question with not an ounce of heat, but she flushed all the same. It seemed she hadn't been fair to him. It had been easier to think of him that way. It hadn't lessened her love for him, just made it simpler to leave. But if there was one thing she did know about her former Master it was that he'd honored his wife. "No, you wouldn't have don't that. I'm sorry. I listened to gossip."

"You listened to Heather," he accused softly. "She's never been my biggest fan, even though I was the one who introduced her to Greg. I did go to the club. I did it out of habit even though it was hard because Cassie loved it. The club was one of the only places she felt perfectly at home. We were married very young. We discovered our sexuality together. She was very submissive, much more than you ever were, pet. Cassie was incredibly soft. Sometimes the world was a bit much for her. I was her protector. I provided for her."

"I'm sure she paid you back." She felt the strange need to defend her predecessor. In defending Cassie, she was almost defending herself. She'd never gotten credit for what she brought to the table.

"She was different than you." His hand was on her knee. Gaby was sure she knew what he was doing. It was a manipulative bastard thing to do, but then that described Cal to a *T*. He was playing with her body, priming her for pleasure. She should get up and walk off, but that would stop him from talking. Cal knew how curious she'd always been. He also knew she was incapable of denying herself this talk.

"How was she different?" She gave up the fight. She relaxed back and let her legs fall open. After all, he was right. He did owe her. His hand immediately took the ceded territory. She felt him sigh as his fingers cupped her mound.

"For one thing, she followed orders." He sounded slightly irritated. His fingers impatiently tugged at the waistband of her panties. "Since when did you start wearing underwear?"

She grinned in the moonlight. Underwear had not been allowed in the Reed-Sullivan household. At least, it hadn't been allowed for her. Cal wore boxers. After she'd left him, buying a six-pack of Hanes for herself was one of the first things she'd done.

"And this feels like cotton." He spoke with the greatest of disdain, as though he could think of nothing worse than plain cotton panties.

"It is." She nearly giggled. She'd forgotten how much fun it was to tease him. She hadn't done it often during their years together, but he'd always handled it well. He was a man who could laugh at himself. "And it's white with little pink daisies."

"Gabrielle." Her name was an admonition.

"Start talking about something important or I'll leave," she swore. He would spend an hour lecturing her on the proper material lingerie should be made from.

"Fine." His fingers simply slid under the offending material. She let her head fall back against his chest as she felt her whole body heating. Watching the scene before had gotten her aroused, but this spiked her sensuality in a way she hadn't felt since long before her operation. It was so good, so right to have his hands on her again. His fingers slid all around her pussy, gently teasing her clit. "I'll let it go for now. Cassie wasn't like you. You're working under the misconception that I chose you because you reminded me of her."

Even under his skillful hands, she tensed at his words. "So you picked me because I didn't remind you of her."

He pinched her clit lightly, making her groan. It had the added effect of forcing her to relax again. His hand went back to its slow slide through her ever-increasing juices. "I picked you because I was crazy about you. Despite what Heather said, I'm not some manwhore screwing every pretty sub to come my way."

"Okay, I'll admit Heather can be a bit over the top. So you didn't go through a bunch of subs?" Gaby asked breathlessly. The night she met him, she'd expected to be one of those subs he scened with and spent time with and left behind. She'd been so attracted to him it hadn't mattered. For her, it was love at first sight. Though it wasn't flattering to think of how desperate she'd been, it was the truth. She'd been willing to take what she could get.

"I did, but not in the way you think." He shifted and she could feel the hard press of his erection against her spine. "About four months after Cassie passed, I went back to the club. It was funny because I didn't want to go back there, but I also couldn't stand the thought of going somewhere else. I knew if I didn't get out, I would go crazy. I met a sub there. I took her up to a private room. She liked to be spanked, so I spanked her. I tied her up, spanked her, and got her off with a vibrator and then I sent her on her way. That was the first night I was able to sleep somewhat. It wasn't perfect, but I wasn't quite as alone as I'd been before. So I found someone else who needed me the next night and the night after that."

"You didn't sleep with them," she said softly, letting the words really permeate her brain. Cal didn't go without sex. He was hardwired to need it. The only nights he hadn't taken her were nights he was away on business. Even then, he would call, complain, and swear he wasn't leaving her behind again.

Because he needed her with him, under him, surrounding him.

"Gabrielle, I've put my cock inside two women my whole life." His mouth was pressed against her ear. "I'm sure that blows my macho image, but it's only been you and Cassie, pet."

"Cal." She couldn't think of what else to say. It didn't make her think less of him. He was an incredible lover.

It appeared he was also very picky.

"Hush," he ordered. He worked two fingers deep inside her, sliding and rubbing her sweet spot. It had been so long that his fingers seemed to fill her up. "God, you're hot. Do you have any idea how much I missed this? What was I saying? Yes, you're different from Cassie. Cassie was much more dependent."

She started to open her mouth, but his thumb brushed firmly against her clit, and she felt the desperate need to push herself against him.

"I know what you would say if you could breathe, pet, but you're wrong. You were dependent on me for money, but that was circumstantial. You were perfectly capable of earning it yourself if you had to. Cassie never held down a job. I married her straight out of high school. I had a trust fund, which came in handy since my family cut me off for marrying a girl they didn't approve of. I didn't come into it right away, and the first years were hard, but eventually I used that fund to put myself through school. Cassie remained in our small apartment. She didn't go to school, and she didn't work. The thought frightened her. Cassie had a bad childhood. She trusted me, but not a lot of other people."

Cal hooked his feet under hers and opened her fully. He growled at the panties in his way but worked around them. His thumb circled her clit as his long fingers fucked deep inside.

"Oh, Cal." The feeling was a revelation. It had been so long since her mind was able to turn off. He slid in and out of her pussy, and she couldn't help but wish it was his cock.

"You're going to come for me," he said, his voice going deep and dark. It wasn't a request. This was the Dom commanding her, and every honey-drenched word reached deep inside her. "How long has it been since you came?"

She didn't even consider lying. It wasn't something she could do when she was in this state. "Ten months, two weeks, and three days."

He chuckled against her ear, the satisfied sound rumbling over her skin. "So no other men then, pet?"

Another finger joined the first two, and she gasped. Her hips were pressing against his hand now as though they had no choice but to move. Her body remembered this rhythm, knew how this was going to go and was desperate for the end of the game.

"No one else." She managed to respond despite the fact that it was getting hard to breathe.

"I don't want anyone else, either," he admitted. "I've been alone since you left me, though I will admit to self-pleasure. Quite a bit of it, actually."

She laughed through her pounding need. He sounded surprisingly sweet as he admitted his masturbatory habits. "I'm glad you had something to get you through."

His fingers slowly rotated, scissoring inside her. His hips moved slightly of their own accord. His erection seemed to swell against her back. It had to be killing him. God, she wanted that cock inside her. She pressed back against him, rubbing against that big dick.

"I thought of you every time I came, Gabrielle. That moment when my balls drew up and I knew I was going to spew everywhere, that's when I saw your face. No matter what I tried to think about, I always saw your face."

His thumb pressed down on her clitoris, and she shouted out. Her cry pierced the quiet night, but she didn't care. Heat and pleasure bloomed across her body like a hot bomb detonating in her womb. She shook slightly and let herself fall back against Callum's chest. He continued to pet her for a moment. Every time his hand slid across her clit was like a little aftershock causing her whole body to shake with pleasure. He seemed to enjoy the effect he had. He nuzzled her neck, pressing kisses there. His cock was rock hard against her back, but he made no move to relieve himself.

"You're so beautiful when you come, Gaby," he whispered against her skin.

"You can't see me." She was facing away from him.

"I don't need to see you. I have it memorized. Your face is perfectly open when you come. Every bit of emotion and pleasure is written there like a book I helped to write. Sometimes I think I like watching you come even more than I like coming myself."

Gaby snorted.

"And I missed that sweet little sound you make when you're terribly amused," he said.

She could feel his smile on her skin.

"I sound like a pig." It was a terrible habit she couldn't stop. Callum had always seemed proper and well-bred, yet he had always loved the way she laughed. His fingers slid out of her pussy, and she bemoaned the loss.

The minute his fingers left her, she found herself on her back in the soft, warm sand. Callum was quick when he was motivated. He loomed over her, his gorgeous face illuminated by the full moon. His lower body covered hers, and he balanced himself on his left hand. With great deliberation, he brought his right hand up to his mouth and painstakingly licked his fingers clean. She could see her cream glistening on his skin just before his tongue came out to lap it up.

"You taste like heaven." He leaned down, sparing her none of his weight. His mouth took hers, his tongue plunging inside like the raider he was.

Gaby gave herself up to the feeling. This was what she craved. His commanding dominance was her weakness. She'd been dominated by other men, but none ever made her feel the way Callum did. She felt all of her trouble flow away. It was always like this when Cal took charge. She could lay back and enjoy because he would take care of her. He would tell her what he liked. He would tell her how much he liked it. She didn't have to worry about being awkward or doing things wrong. Cal would gently push her the way he needed her to go and praise her when she got there.

She let her arms drift up and around his neck. Her tongue came out to play with his, and he growled his appreciation. She could taste her tangy arousal on his lips as he slanted his mouth over hers. His erection nudged insistently at her soaking pussy. He spread her legs wide, leaving nowhere for her to hide from him. He was in control. Now she remembered why she hadn't worn panties around this man. They were constantly wet.

"Gabrielle?" Her name was now a question. His eyes were oddly uncertain as he looked down on her.

"Come inside me, Cal." She knew he had promised to keep it in his pants, but there was no way she didn't want him deep inside her. Her pussy cried out for him. Even though she'd recently come, she already ached for him again. He was only here for a week. They

71

should make the most of it.

"You'll marry me, then?"

It was like a bucket of cold water had been thrown on her head. "What?"

"I asked you to marry me," he said. His face was a mask of desire. His hips pumped against her while he spoke, his dick sliding over her clit, making her crazy. But his slacks and her panties were in between them, and it appeared he was leaving them there for now. "I deserve an answer."

"You're a bastard." She was already hot and bothered again and a part of her pleaded to give him the words he wanted so he would fuck her. If she said yes, he would open his slacks, rip her panties off, and be inside her before she could think straight. Her pussy seemed to think that was a great plan.

"Probably." He ground his cock against her, swiveling his hips so he hit her desperate clit just the right way. "But I am a bastard with standards. I have no intention of having a brief affair with you, Gabrielle. I don't want fast sex. I want commitment. I was uninterested in an affair before. It's why I had you sign a contract with me."

He'd been damn insistent about his contract. She tried to move against him, but he held her still. He was torturing her. He knew exactly which spot to hit to tantalize and tease. She was incredibly close, but sex wouldn't solve their problems. "You didn't want marriage then. You were very clear about it."

"Well, if I had realized how little you thought of the contract between us, perhaps I would have insisted," Cal mused. His face was flushing, his breath becoming ragged. Gaby knew all the signs. He was getting close to coming. "Gabrielle, seriously, admit you'll marry me. I can't hold out much longer. Come on. We both would rather I be inside you when I come. I want it so fucking much. I need to be inside you."

"I'm not marrying you," she insisted. In this, she was going to be in charge and not her libido. She squirmed, trying to get out from under him.

"Don't do that, pet," he ordered, but it was too late. He gasped and gave in. He pressed his cock against her pussy and groaned as he released all over his expensive slacks. He pumped against her over and over, his whole body shaking. His head fell forward, his lips nuzzling against her neck.

Gaby was able to roll him off her. That's what righteous indignation could do for a girl. She got to her feet and barely restrained herself from kicking sand in his face. He sprawled across the sand like a satisfied warrior. There was an arrogant grin on his face as he looked up at her. He took deep breaths of the humid air and made no move to come after her.

"You're an asshole, Callum."

He grinned up at her. "But I'm your asshole, Gabrielle. Speaking of assholes. I've missed yours, pet. Oh, how I've missed it. I would really like to tunnel my way in again. You're so tight around my cock. Remember how good it feels with me buried in your tight little ass while I fuck your pussy with a vibrator?"

She felt a fresh wave of arousal coat her pussy. "Damn you."

She stalked off.

"You'll marry me, Gabrielle."

His words carried across the sand as she practically ran from him. The trouble was, she couldn't be sure they weren't true.

Chapter Four

Callum stretched and yawned when the knock came. He looked at the door, suspicious of who would be requesting entry at such an early hour. It was barely nine a.m. That was an indecent hour at a place like this. Decadence was a club that partied until the wee hours of the morning. This was not a rise and shine place.

Still, he had gone to bed early. He wasn't here to party, and once Gabrielle had run away, he'd gone to his lonely bed.

Cal rolled off the mattress and shrugged into one of the plush robes the resort offered its guests. He crossed the room in four long strides. His hand gripped the handle, and he hoped Gabrielle had changed her mind. Maybe it was his sweet sub on the other side of the door and she'd come to surrender. Perhaps she'd tossed and turned the way he had and come to the conclusion that she couldn't sleep without him beside her. Hell, he'd had that revelation the day after she'd left him. He felt a smile spread across his face at the thought.

And then he frowned.

The man standing in his doorway with a tray in front of him was decidedly not Gabrielle. "I did not order room service."

Nor did he enjoy surprises.

The man with the tray was brisk and efficient and seemed not a bit put off by Cal's dark tone. He smiled, though Cal could see it didn't reach his eyes. "All part of the VIP service, sir. My manager asked me to bring you coffee. She says you take it black. There is also an assortment of croissants and muffins she thought you might enjoy."

So that was her game. Cal opened the door wide. "Tell your boss it's a nice gesture, but I'll still be in the dining room this morning. I have a sudden urge for an omelet. I'll be there for lunch and dinner as well. She can't avoid me."

The waiter pushed the cart through the door and gave Cal what he considered an entirely unprofessional once-over. From the expression on the other man's face, Cal could see he wasn't impressed.

He considered the man entering his room. He was a bit under six feet, giving Cal the clear height advantage. He wore neatly pressed khaki slacks and a crisp white polo. His haircut was expensive and suited his thick dark brown hair. He seemed a bit young. Cal found himself quickly sizing the man up as a sexual rival. It was all about the look in the man's green eyes. He didn't like Cal, and that probably meant he knew exactly who he was to Gabrielle. The only reasonable explanation was that this employee had a problem with Cal's relationship with his boss. He closed the door and waited to see what the waiter would do.

The younger man neatly poured out a cup of delicious-smelling coffee. "I wish you wouldn't."

"Wouldn't what?"

"Go to the dining room." The waiter's voice was civil but chilly. He offered Cal the coffee.

Cal took it. He could use some caffeine. He was going back into battle and it looked like his first skirmish was happening right here in his room. "I'll have to disappoint you then. Do you mind giving me your name? It's only fair since you seem to be willing to advise me about my dining choices."

"It has nothing to do with your eating preferences, Mr. Reed. I'm Cody Linwood." Having done his duty, Cody faced Callum. "I know all about your relationship with Gaby. I don't appreciate what you're doing to her now."

Cal took a drink of the strong coffee. It was perfect. Cal recognized it as the brand Greg served in his own home, so he knew it was the best money could buy. "If you're going to try to pass yourself off as her lover, let me warn you I won't believe you, and I won't take it well."

75

Cody laughed. "Gabrielle is my friend. She's not my lover. I'm afraid she's not my type."

Cal suppressed a smile. So not a sexual rival at all. Who the man must be fell into place. "Forgive me. You must be the nurse Greg hired. I appreciate everything you've done for Gaby. But I have no intention of leaving this island without her. Nothing you say or do is going to change my mind."

Cody's foot tapped, a sign Cal took as impatience. "I was with her when she came out of surgery, you know."

The coffee turned to ash in his mouth. He put the mug on the counter. He said the only thing he could think to say. "I wish I had been there."

"At the time, I did as well. It was odd. I worked with her before her surgery, prepping her and getting her ready. She didn't mention a lover at all. Her friend was with her, but other than that, I thought she was alone. And then she actually had the surgery. She cried for you when she came out of the anesthesia. She was in so much pain. She was confused, and she called out for you over and over again. I had to ask Heather who she meant. The way she said your name…well, I would have done anything to ease that ache. It was something I couldn't fix with morphine."

Cal felt his hands clenching. He attempted to keep his face still, but his chest felt too small, his eyes on the edge of becoming blurry. "I didn't know."

It felt like an excuse. He should have gone after her. Somehow should have known something was wrong, something that went beyond her given reason. He should never have accepted his dismissal.

Cody's eyes softened slightly. "I know, but you have to wonder why she chose not to tell you. She didn't trust you. Just because she wants you doesn't mean you're good for her."

Callum's first instinct was to pick up the smaller man bodily and toss him over the balcony. He took a deep breath. That probably wouldn't further his cause with Gabrielle. "We were both being very stubborn at the time. I thought she was manipulating me."

"She probably was," Cody conceded. "She's not the saint everyone thinks she is. Gaby comes off as very soft and sweet. Then

76

you listen to her chewing out one of our vendors or watch her deal with an unruly guest."

"She can take a strip out of your hide, that's for sure." Cal smiled, remembering one particular phone conversation he'd overheard when she'd discovered one of the contractors he'd hired to renovate the bathroom was overcharging them. She'd been patient for a while, but when she didn't get her way, she'd cussed a blue streak. He'd been standing outside the office, listening in as she dealt with the man. He'd been quite proud of the way she refused to back down and got everything she deserved.

He hadn't mentioned it to her. He'd pretended not to have heard a thing. It would be a turning point in their relationship. If they'd acknowledged how strong she was, he would have been forced to admit that she was something beyond a submissive to him. He would have accepted her as a partner, and he hadn't been ready for that.

He wasn't sure he was ready now, but he didn't seem to have a choice.

Cody's eyes narrowed. "I'm surprised you know about Gaby's temper. I thought she played a role with you."

"Oh, she did, indeed." He gestured to one of the elegant seats that formed the intimate parlor of the suite. He sat down on the sofa, willing to try the coffee again. Cody accepted a seat, and Callum continued in a civilized fashion. "She pretended to be perfectly submissive, but I knew from the beginning it was a bit of an act. Gabrielle likes to be told what to do during sex. She craves it. Like many very strong females, she almost needs permission to allow herself to let go. Submission gives this to her."

Cody waved his explanations away. "Yes, I know this. I'm not a tourist. The question is, why did you allow her to pretend to be twenty-four seven with you?"

Callum shrugged. He'd thought about this quite a bit. God knew he'd spent a good portion of the last year going over what had gone wrong with Gabrielle. "It wasn't pretend. She really was while we were together. I thought, at the time, she could be happy like that. Like all relationships, we evolved. It happened slowly, so slowly I didn't notice or told myself it wasn't important. I can see now that I was gradually giving up control as I became more comfortable in the

77

relationship. At first, I kept everything very separate. She was kept at home. I had my office and work. They were completely separate things. And then one day, I wanted to see her for lunch. So I went home. I started doing that more and more. Then when I couldn't get away, I asked her to come to me. That's how she met my staff. Slowly she started to come to work functions and she was a part of my daily life then. And my night life. And my every moment. By the end, Gabrielle had taken over the accounting for my law practice. She ran the household. She ran my life. I was the one pretending to still be in control."

"Is that why you refused to marry her?"

The coffee mug came down on the end table more forcefully than Cal intended. "That is none of your business."

Cody gave no sign he noticed Cal's loss of temper. "I disagree. It's my job to keep her healthy. Part of that is to keep her spirits up. I've been an oncology nurse for six years, Mr. Reed. Medicine is only a part of a patient's recovery. Gabrielle's will and spirit are very important. I've managed to keep her calm and focused up until roughly two weeks ago. Our meditation sessions have gone to crap since she came back from Dallas."

"Meditation?"

"And yoga," Cody replied. He seemed ready for Cal to deride him. "Meditation has been found to help cancer patients. It alleviates fatigue and increases positive thoughts. Laugh all you like, but I believe it helps."

"I am not laughing," Cal said quietly. "Gabrielle believes this?"

"Yes."

"But she's still taking her medication?"

Cody rolled his eyes. "Yes, of course. The meditation works in tandem with the current protocols. I'm not some flake trying to convince her we can solve cancer by holding hands and chanting. However, I do believe that keeping her spirits up is intensely important. Her will needs to be focused on her health and well being. She needs positive influences and energy flowing her way. It's why I came here to ask you to leave."

"I can't." Cal was surprised at the longing he heard in his own voice. He cleared his throat self-consciously. "I don't mean to disrupt

Gabrielle's life. I mean to set it back on an even keel. She was wrong to leave me. She was absolutely wrong to lie to me about why she was leaving. I could have helped her enormously through this."

Cody's eyes were sharp on him, his jaw tight. "And when the time came to make the decision to take her breasts? How would you have helped then? Gaby was a plaything to you. Would you really have advised her to lop those gorgeous breasts off? I've seen pictures. I've also heard the stories. I know you used to parade her around that club of yours and show off her lovely body. She has scars now."

Cal was on his feet, unable to contain his anger. "Listen, you little shit, I couldn't care less that my Gabrielle has scars. It wouldn't have been an issue. There wouldn't have been a discussion or a moment's anxiety that she was making the wrong decision. She wouldn't have been alone and vulnerable and worried. I would have told her what I wanted. I would have told her I wanted those things off her body and that I wouldn't care if she didn't reconstruct them at all. I would have told her she's beautiful whether or not she has breasts. She would have gone into that surgery with the complete understanding that her Master thought she was the most beautiful thing on the planet and always would be."

Cody held his ground. His arms went across his chest as he stared at Cal for a moment. "Now that, I didn't expect."

Cal huffed and found himself pacing. "And what did you expect? That I would charge in, take one look at her scars, and run away?"

A rueful smile crossed Cody's face. "I suppose I did. I don't have a very high opinion of you."

"Join the crowd."

The nurse shrugged. "Would it help to know my opinion is changing?"

"Gabrielle's opinion is the only one that matters." Cal crossed to the windows that overlooked the ocean. The waves just kept rolling in. He took a deep breath and allowed the sound to calm him a bit. He could understand why Gaby was happy here. It was very peaceful. He heard Cody get up behind him. "That hurt the most. I know I'm not supposed to be hurt, but I can't stop how I feel. I wasn't allowed to perform my primary function."

"Primary function? As a Dom?"

79

"As a Dom. As the man who cared for her. Even if she'd seen me as a friend she would have allowed me to be there. That was my function. To be beside her. I was shut out of the one thing I might have been good at—taking care of her. I wonder where we would be if that pain had been ours and not merely hers, if she'd shared that part of her life with me."

"You're acting like it was a good part."

"No. I understand that, but isn't sharing the bad parts really the measure of a true couple? I didn't think about it at the time. I guess no one ever does, but the fact that she wouldn't share that dark moment with me…it makes me ache in a way I never thought I would." His mind was bouncing around, seeking a way to ease the pain he found inside him. Perhaps there was one. She couldn't shut him out of everything. "Would you teach me?"

"Teach you what?" The nurse sounded a bit surprised.

"To meditate."

"Why?"

Cal turned and regarded the man who served as Gabrielle's confidant. It was a role he hoped to take over. "I don't know if it works, but some people think positive energy can be healing. If Gabrielle believes this, then why can't I add mine to hers?"

She couldn't stop him from praying for her, from asking the universe to give her all the health and healing she deserved. That was still his right and he could honor her by doing it her way.

The nurse's entire face softened. "All right. Why don't you go put on a pair of sweatpants or something comfortable? I'll show you a few techniques. How long do you intend to stay?"

"As long as it takes." Cal's reply was sure.

Cody laughed. "Then I should have plenty of time to teach you."

* * * *

Gaby stared at her admin. It was late in the day. Dinner was being served in the main dining room, but then that was kind of the point of being here in the office. She was avoiding being in whatever space Cal was in. That had been the whole point of her day—stay away from Cal. Apparently Cal had ideas of how to spend his time, too. She stood over Jackie's desk and felt her eyes narrow and her heart rate speed up. It took a moment to let the words sink in.

"I'm sorry, he did what?"

Jackie swallowed once, and then twice, before finally answering. Her eyes were distinctly owl-like behind her glasses. "Mr. Reed came in earlier and asked for the financials. He wanted to review the P&L and wanted to see a detailed accounting of capital expenditures. He also wanted to review the Fuller file."

The Fuller file was an in-depth description of the only lawsuit she'd had to deal with since she'd taken over the resort. It was a minor annoyance, something every hotel had to deal with. A guest had slipped in the hall coming in from the pool. Gaby knew her staff had done everything they should have done. It was just a question of settling because the legal fees of fighting a suit like that would likely be more than simply settling. Why the hell would Callum need to look through her books and read a file on an open lawsuit? He was supposed to be a guest. Guests didn't come into the management office to make sure their former subs were performing adequately.

Unless Greg had sent him in to evaluate her performance. Was this going to be his revenge on her? Was he going to send back a report that stated she was unsuitable in her job?

"And you gave it to him?" Gaby was aware her voice had taken on a distinctly menacing tone. Her admin looked startled.

"I…he asked for them." Jackie's hands twisted in her lap. Her brown eyes were suddenly watery behind the lenses of her glasses.

Gaby gave herself a second to check the anger that was threatening to bubble over. It wasn't really Jackie's fault. Cal could be very intimidating when he wanted to be. He was probably furious with her for ignoring him all day. It was obvious Cal was on a power trip. She couldn't hold her poor admin accountable. "Okay. He came in and threatened you. I will handle him, Jackie. I am sorry you had to deal with that."

Jackie shook her head, and a dreamy smile crossed her face. "Oh, no, Gaby. He was really nice. He asked if you were in, and when I told him you weren't, he looked so sad. I think he likes you."

The last bit was said with a sigh, as though Jackie really envied her. It set Gaby's teeth on edge. "So you turned over our financials to him because you were worried he had a broken heart?"

More than likely, she'd turned them over because he had startlingly piercing blue eyes and a devastating smile.

Jackie took a moment. She seemed a bit confused. "I thought Mr. Hall sent him."

Yes, she was a bit worried about that herself. "I would have informed you if Mr. Hall had sent someone to review our finances."

Unless he'd had a reason to send someone in without telling his manager.

For a moment, Jackie seemed to be getting the notion that she had done something wrong. She sat up straight in her chair and sucked her bottom lip between her teeth. She shook it off and gave Gaby an encouraging smile. "I don't think he's out to do anything bad. He seems like such a nice man. When he ordered in lunch, he asked me what I wanted, too. He even made coffee for me. Isn't that nice? Such a nice man wouldn't do anything bad."

"You should be glad you live on an island, Jackie. You would be horribly murdered by the first serial killer to come along."

Gaby turned and strode out of her office. She checked the clock in the hall. It was almost eight. Cal had requested a table for two in the main dining room at eight o'clock. Gaby had no doubt that he'd been sure she would be sitting across from him. This whole episode with the financial data was Callum's way of forcing her to meet with him.

He would call her up in a bit and hold it over her head. *Hey, I saw some of the reports and would like to talk about them with you. No is not an acceptable answer.*

It was just like him. He couldn't possibly take no for an answer. She'd spent the entire day avoiding him. He'd shown up to her meditation hour and sat down beside her, offering to hold her hands in his. He'd said something about adding his energy to hers, and she'd fled. It had been too close to what she wanted from him.

It was ridiculous to think he even knew what her meditation time meant. He thought all that metaphysical shit was nothing but people trying to explain away the universe. She'd heard it from him more than once so she hadn't fallen for his crap when he'd tried that on her.

Since that time, his number had popped up on her phone three times an hour. Her voice mail was full. After the fiasco on the beach the night before, Gaby had decided that the only way to keep her hands off Callum was to avoid him altogether.

He was only here for a week, and then he would retreat back to his precious law office. There was no way he would stay away from work for too long. She knew deep down that he didn't intend to stay here for a whole week. He thought he could snap his fingers and give her those intense looks of his and she would be on the next plane to Vegas with him. He would, no doubt, sign all the paperwork the cheapo wedding chapel would require, and then he would fuck her hard for a few days while they were on vacation and take her home and set her back on a shelf. He would take her down when he needed her, and he would forget about her the rest of the time.

He'd said he thought about her always. The words floated through her brain. Cal never lied to her, even when it would hurt her to know the truth. Oh, she didn't doubt he fudged a bit about jeans that didn't particularly flatter her, but then that wasn't something that mattered to Cal. This would matter to him.

No. He was merely trying to get her under control. He couldn't find her today, so he was letting her know he would cause trouble if she tried to avoid him again. Damn him. He was trying to use her business to force her hand. He would find out exactly who he was dealing with.

She wasn't some scared, mad-in-love sub anymore. She'd been forced to be strong, and he was going to find out that she'd come through the fire a different person.

She strode into the elegant dining room, completely ignoring the people who stared at her. Yep, she definitely stood out among the well-dressed diners. This evening was a black-tie dinner. The elegant, Asian-inspired, five-course meal was being served by efficient, discreet waiters and waitresses.

Nothing ever shocked this group. Well, nothing sexual. But now they all stopped to look at her because politeness and social niceties mattered. She was dressed in cutoff jean shorts, a slightly dirty white T-shirt, and sneakers. She was sure her hair looked a mess because she'd spent the day working on the resort's docks. It was the one place Cal would never expect her to be.

83

Though she'd tried to clean up in the bathroom in her office, she'd been distracted by the news that Cal was checking into her accounting.

They might be shocked at the sight of her, but she wasn't putting this confrontation off so she could dress up for them.

She spotted him across the room. Of course, he had the best table in the house. Cal wouldn't settle for less. And he had replaced her. He was sitting in his tux talking to someone else. It looked like a man. They sat together at the table overlooking the magnificent Caribbean. Cal laughed. His dark head was thrown back before he continued to speak to his companion, and something broke inside her. He was having a grand old time while she was worried sick. Story of their life together.

As she walked up the four stairs that took her to the upper dining area, Cal looked over. He saw her, and a smile broke across his face. His eyes lit up, and she saw him mouth the word "Gabrielle."

He looked at her like she was the sun in the sky. It momentarily threw her off because she'd never stopped to study how his face changed when she walked in a room, how his eyes warmed and suddenly the air wasn't chilly around him. Then Cal's companion turned.

"Hello, G," Cody said with a grin.

Or Cal was simply very good a manipulating her and all that romantic shit was crap rattling around in her head. This, this was real. Her best friend was sitting with the enemy. "How could you?"

Cody's green eyes widened. "How could I what? Look this fabulous? It isn't easy, G. It starts with amazing genetics…"

Gaby practically growled at him. "You know how I feel about him. How could you sit here with him after everything he's done to me?"

"What exactly have I done, Gabrielle?" Cal's voice was flat. His smile was gone. It was completely irrational, but for a moment, she wished it would come back. "I understand I was a fool before, but I would like to be judged for my actions when I finally had all the facts. I have cared for you. I put my life on hold to follow you and try to mend our relationship. I hoped to spend the day with you. When you refused to answer my calls, I stepped back because I knew you needed space. What about any of that do you find fault with?"

She felt her mouth turn down. Stubborn pride welled up inside her, causing her to stand a little straighter. He wasn't turning this around on her. "Oh, yeah, Cal. You really took a step back. You went to my admin and requested my books. You spent the whole afternoon spying on me. How dare you?"

"Uhmm, Gaby. Let's calm down. You're making a bit of a scene, dear." Cody looked around the room.

Cal's fingers were drumming along the table. He completely ignored Cody, choosing to stare at her with icy eyes. "When it became obvious you were going to great lengths to put distance between us because you're afraid to be alone with me…"

Gaby practically screeched. "Afraid!"

"Yes, pet. There's only one reason you would spend an entire day running from me." Cal kept his voice quiet. Now his eyes roamed around, taking in the crowd that was surely watching them. "You're afraid because you know I can have you on your back with your legs spread, begging me to fuck you. Relax. I mean to give you time."

"Oh, yes. That's why you went to my admin and tricked her into giving you my books. You were giving me time. Sure." Gaby pointed her index finger at him and did nothing to lower her voice.

"Tricked?"

"Gaby, seriously, why don't you sit down?" Cody looked around the dining room. Gaby could see his embarrassment rising, but he'd betrayed her by dining with the enemy. He was supposed to be on her side. "We can have dinner, and Cal can tell you all about his new investment."

The last thing she wanted was to sit and hear about all of Cal's business dealings. She wasn't his sub anymore. She didn't have to care. "I don't care about his new investment. I want him gone. I'm going to call security."

Cal took a deep breath. "I am being patient, Gabrielle. If you don't want to talk tonight, then I'll wait. If you don't want to talk tomorrow, then I'll wait. If seeing me in the dining room upsets you, then I'll go back to my suite and eat there alone."

His refusal to fight was making her crazy. She wanted…she wasn't sure what she wanted, but it wasn't for Cal to walk off the battlefield. Something nasty rolled around in her head. Seeing him, being close to him, was bringing back all the feelings she'd ever had about him. This man had been her everything and he had broken her in a way no one and nothing else could. Perhaps the only way to truly get him out of her head was to utterly break the relationship. Not the soft way she'd done it before, but by burning down everything around them. She wanted him as pissed off as she was. "You'll leave my resort, and you'll do it tonight."

Cal's hands fisted, his jaw tightening. "Sit down before you make a complete fool of yourself."

"You're the one who's made a fool of himself," she shot back. "That information you stole was proprietary. You aren't this resort's lawyer. We have a lawyer in Bridgetown. I could have you disbarred. How would that be for you? You think you're so high and mighty that you can get away with anything, but I'll show you."

Cal sat back, the look of pure satisfaction on his face sending a chill through her system. "You also, as of three days ago, have a new owner, Miss Sullivan."

She took a step back, the truth flooding her system. What had happened? Greg wouldn't do this to her. He knew how important this place was to her. He wouldn't let Cal buy in and have control of her job. Control of her. This had become her place. She'd found some semblance of power and peace here. "No. Greg would have told me. Heather would have told me."

"Heather doesn't know. I asked Greg to keep it quiet." Cal stood up. He sighed and held his hand out. "Please sit down and join us. I was just talking to Cody about how to tell you. I bought in because Greg explained how much it means to you."

But she wasn't listening. She heard what he said, but all that went through her brain was that he had never taken the time to bring her here. She remembered the pictures he had in boxes in his closet of him and his wife here at this resort. They would have the resort photographer take elaborate photos of him and his lovely wife. If there was a photo of herself and Cal, it was likely on someone's phone or stored in a digital cloud somewhere. It hadn't been framed and mounted in their home like a declaration of the love of the owners. There weren't any pictures of them on vacation because they'd never gone, certainly never here. He'd brought Cassie, but he hadn't found the time to bring her. He hadn't thought of this place associated with anyone but his Cassie until he needed to control Gaby.

Thinking only of wiping that inviting smile off his face, she picked up his two fingers of fifteen-year-old Scotch and threw it in his face.

She knew it was a mistake the minute she did it. The glass fell from her hand, and she stood stock-still for a moment. Her eyes finally took in what her friend had tried to warn her about. Everyone in the dining room was watching. They'd likely heard there was a new owner and now the manager had publically humiliated him.

Her volcanic anger seemed to deflate in a heartbeat. What had she been thinking? Why had she pushed him? "Callum, I am sorry."

"Not as sorry as you're going to be, pet." He calmly used his linen napkin to wipe the Scotch from his face. He looked down at his formerly immaculate dress shirt and silk bow tie. He shook his head as he pulled the tie off and tossed it on the table.

Gaby took an all-important step back. It was past time to calm down and deal with this situation like adults. Cal was too still. He was dangerous when he went still and his voice was soft and calm. "You're right. We need to sit down and talk about this."

"Do you think for a second that all these nice people aren't getting on their phones and texting their friends about the scene you just performed," Cal said, his voice dead calm.

Shit, she was in trouble. "I'll publically apologize."

Because while the theme might be swingers' weekend, there were a whole lot of lifestylers here, too, who had witnessed the big bad Dom get humiliated.

"It won't work. Public punishment is the only way this ends. Don't worry. This crowd will simply consider it a dinner show."

Gaby turned to run, but he was on her in an instant. Before she could make it down the steps, he hauled her up and over his shoulder. Her ass was high in the air, and he smacked it soundly.

That wasn't a playful smack. She felt that one all along her spine. Pain flared. "Asshole! Put me down."

Cal smacked her other cheek, lighting it up just as hard. "You'll get one for each and every time you curse at me, pet. When you add it to the punishment you're about to get for embarrassing me and yourself in front of our guests, you're in for a rough night."

Gaby looked to Cody, who was standing by the table. "Call security."

He shrugged. "He's actually the boss, G. I don't think security will toss him out. You should probably use your safe word."

He shouted that from across the room because Cal was moving quickly. Gaby had no illusions as to where he was going. Cal had helped design the play areas of the resort. He knew his way to the dungeon. He would probably know it blindfolded.

"Would it work?" Gaby asked, relaxing against him. There was no point in fighting him. Kicking and scratching would simply get her in more trouble.

"I will always honor your safe word, Gabrielle." He stopped at the bottom of the stairs that led to the dungeon. "Are you going to use it?"

All she had to do was say the word "red" and everything would stop. Cal would place her on her feet and walk away. One little word and he'd probably leave the island altogether. She had never said the word to him. She had studiously avoided it, even in their normal lives. "No, you bastard. I'm not using it."

His hand slapped her ass again, and he started up the stairs.

Everything fell into place and she acknowledged why she'd done what she did. *This* was why she'd pushed him. She'd pushed him because she couldn't ask for what she wanted. She'd pushed him because she was in a corner and didn't know how to get out. All day long she'd thought about him even as she'd avoided him. She'd thought about this, connecting with him one last time, one last scene to end it all.

She couldn't go back to him. She couldn't be with him the way she had been before. Too much had happened. But she wanted this. Her whole body craved him. Even as the cheeks of her ass burned from the sting of his hands, she knew she was wet and ready to take more.

Cal kicked open the door to the dungeon, paying the man at the small desk no heed. From her perch against Cal's back, she glimpsed the security guard hustle up from his desk and follow them into the room.

"Miss Sullivan? Is that you?" The guard sounded shocked, but then it wasn't every day she entered the dungeon, much less got her ass dragged into it.

Cal whirled around, and her world shifted. She couldn't see the guard anymore. She stared at the back of Cal's shirt. The smell of expensive Scotch still clung to the fabric.

"I would suggest you back off." Cal's voice was low and tight. She'd pushed him way too far and he was coiled and ready to strike.

"Look, Mr. Whatever your name is. She's my boss and I won't let her be mistreated."

"Glen..." she started, but a swift smack stopped the next words before they left her mouth.

"We're in a dungeon, pet. Remember your manners. I did not give you leave to speak. As to you, Glen, she is my sub, and I'll have your head if you try to come between us."

"Hey, Glen." A new voice broke through the tension. Gaby craned to look up. Her dungeon monitor, a Dom named James, was hurrying across the room. "Is there a problem here?"

"He has Gaby," Glen replied, sounding unsure.

"Has she said her safe word?" James asked.

"No."

"Then back off," James barked. "And, Glen, that's Callum Reed. He's part owner of the place now. He walks in this dungeon, you give him what he wants."

Cal was walking again. She wondered if he'd take her to a privacy room or if he intended to chain her up in the main dungeon. "Does everyone know you bought in except me?"

"I asked Greg not to tell you. I talked to James earlier today. That's the only reason he knows. I wanted to make sure the dungeon was well-stocked and that I still understood all the protocols." He smacked her ass again, the sound cracking through the dungeon. "And I didn't give you permission to open that mouth."

He sat her down on her feet in front of a padded sawhorse. "Take off your clothes, Gabrielle."

Her hands immediately went to her chest. Pure panic threatened to boil over at the thought of being naked. There weren't many people in the dungeon, but later, there would be some. Even the swingers liked to come play down here. They would all look at her. They would all see her scars and she would watch them turn away.

Including Cal.

Cal took the choice from her. He hauled her up and pushed her across the sawhorse, her chest on the padded back. Her ass was off the apparatus, and Cal efficiently tied her hands together under the bar.

"Do you need a gag?"

"No, asshole." She spat out the response, her fear fleeing because he couldn't get her shirt off now. She was nestled against the sawhorse, her scars safe, so it was all right to spit bile and vitriol his way. The truth was she needed this.

She needed this badly and he was going to give it to her.

Gaby pulled at the expertly tied restraints. He'd used a silk scarf he'd grabbed from the table near the apparatus. The dungeon had been set up for the night. There was a tray of neatly placed restraints ranging from rope to handcuffs. Cal always preferred silk. Her hands were tied palms together. The knot was tight, but not so tight that she would lose circulation.

Cal's eyes were dark when he kneeled and looked up at her. "Not another word, unless it's your safe word. I've been indulgent up to this point."

Indulgent? Her ass was on fire. Unfortunately, it was on fire in a way that also had her pussy pulsing. She relaxed against the padding and let her cheek rest. The wall in front of her was mirrored, and she could watch Cal work. The first thing he did was request a knife from Master James, who was more than happy to provide it.

Damn it. She was going to make him replace her shorts. He might have all the money in the world for clothes, but she didn't. Not that she said a word. She wasn't afraid, merely excited as she watched him carefully cut the denim from her body. Her pulse ticked up at the thought of getting what she wanted without having to give in to Cal's ridiculous demands. She watched as he sighed when he saw the white cotton panties she wore. Two flicks of the knife and they joined the shorts on the floor. Cal pulled off her shoes, and she was naked from the waist down. The sight of her naked ass in the air made her feel vulnerable and got her heart to pounding.

"Thank you, James." Cal handed the dungeon monitor his knife but made no move to dismiss him.

Gaby felt herself flush slightly. James McKnight was her employee. Greg had hired him years ago, and he'd been one of the people she had come to rely on. Now, he was admiring her ass.

"It's quite lovely, isn't it?" Cal ran his hand across her cheeks. His finger slid lightly down the seam of her ass.

"She's very fair." There was a slight hesitation in the Dom's voice.

"Gabrielle." Cal's voice was commanding. "Your employee is worried about your welfare. He doesn't know who I am beyond the fact that I own a piece of this club and I strode in here and promptly tied up his boss. Will you please explain to him what you call me when we're alone?"

There was only one answer to that. She might not call him that anymore, but she would tonight. "Master."

"I always knew she was a sub. Careful with that one." James laughed, the sound very friendly to her ears. "She will top from the bottom. Really, though, it's the only way to go. You want a sub who knows what she wants. What's life without a power struggle?"

"Boring," Cal said, surprising her. She sighed as Cal slid his hand across her backside. "Tell me something, Master James. What do you think of my pretty sub?"

"I think I'd like to fuck her very much. She's lovely, Master Callum."

Gaby watched as a slow smile spread across Callum's handsome face. He'd always liked to show her off. "Yes, she is. She's gorgeous, and she's mine. How long do I have before we have a large audience?"

"Not long." James looked at his watch. "Dinner should be over soon. Some of the swingers will come down here. More once they realize a hot D/s scene is being played out."

"Then I should get on with it." He selected a quarter-inch round cane from the wall of canes, floggers, paddles, and whips. He tested it against his palm then immediately brought it against her naked ass.

Gaby started at the pain. Fire licked across her skin. She gasped but managed not to yell. The pain bloomed into her flesh, causing tears to form. She looked at Cal in the mirror. He stood over her, cane in hand, and despite the pain, despite the heartbreak, she couldn't help but admit to herself that she loved him.

"You do not air our private differences in public, pet."

The cane came down on the opposite cheek. She bit her lip to keep from crying out. An aching warmth was building deep inside her, spreading outward from the burning sensation.

"You should have stayed, Gabrielle. You had no right to leave me." His voice was filled with anger. She could see his face was flushed as he struck her again, this time on her thighs. As always, the pain bloomed outward and then flowered into a jagged form of pleasure. "I would have stood by you. I would have taken care of you. Damn it, it was my right to take care of you."

Cal moved behind her. He kicked gently at her feet, spreading her legs, and his hand moved between them. Her eyes nearly rolled to the back of her head with pleasure at his first touch. So long. It had been so damn long since she'd felt this way, since she'd sunk into submission and let this man have his way. For some reason it was only Cal who could give this to her, and she feared it would always be this way. His fingers slid through her arousal. "That's what I want. I want this little pussy wet and begging for me."

It took everything Gaby had not to groan. It felt so good. His fingers played, splitting her labia and exploring, lighting up her every nerve ending. He teased her clit, running his finger just across it only to pull back and plunge into her pussy. The sound of her pussy sucking at his fingers filled the room. A whimper came from her throat. She didn't want his fingers. She wanted his cock. She wanted him to shove that big cock of his deep inside and ride her until she couldn't think anymore.

His hand left her, and it was a mere second before it came down again on her ass. Tears blurred Gaby's vision. She was sore. She needed so much.

"That was for ruining a perfectly good glass of Scotch."

She heard murmurs from the small crowd now gathering around. She glanced up, looking at them in the mirror. They were shaking their heads in general agreement that she deserved to be punished for spilling a truly good single malt. At least ten people were standing around now, some men and some women. The fact that they were here wouldn't stop Cal. Gaby had been with him long enough to know that they wouldn't bother Cal as long as they followed the rules of the dungeon. As long as the people currently watching her stayed quiet and didn't interrupt him, he'd fuck her in front of a thousand people. It wouldn't bother Gaby either, as long as her shirt stayed on. What *was* bothering Gaby was an overwhelming need to come.

Cal took a step back. In the mirror, she watched as he admired the marks he'd placed on her ass. He ran his hand across them, tracing the pink lines he found there. They would be gone by morning and she would miss them. Cal was always, always careful with her. He'd never raised a welt. He knew exactly how much pressure to exert to make the pain erotic. He leaned over, his blue eyes hot as he kissed each cheek. He turned back to the row of toys and unwrapped a medium-sized anal plug.

Oh god, he was going to do it. Her whole body tensed at the idea that he was going to play with her ass. It had been too long since he'd filled her ass. It would burn and hurt all over again, just as it had when she was a virgin there. Her torture wasn't over. Not even close.

He poured lube over the plug, greasing it. When he parted the cheeks of her ass, she shivered, though not from the cold.

"Push out when I tell you to. Do not disobey me or this plug will be all you get."

She was too far gone to argue with him. Everything she wanted was right there and she wasn't going to give him a reason to pick up the cane again. She bit back a groan as she felt him fit the head of the plug against her anus.

Cal swatted her sore ass. "Don't tense."

Deep breath. She filled her lungs once and then again, trying to relax when her whole body was on edge. Cal pushed the plug, forcing her anus to open to take it.

"Press back. That's it. Such a pretty little asshole."

Another deep breath and she tried to flatten the small of her back, pressing out against the plug. She shivered at the sensation as the plug slid home. When Cal slapped her ass this time, every nerve clenched around the plug, a jangled cacophony of pain and pleasure.

He walked around and ran a hand through her hair. "Do not try my patience again, pet. Next time, I will not go easy. Next time, I'll have you on a St. Andrew's Cross counting out forty lashes of a single tail. I'll pull you down and fuck your mouth, and you will not be allowed to come all night. Is that understood?"

She nodded, hoping he wouldn't put the "no coming" punishment on her this evening.

Cal's hands went to his belt, and he shoved his slacks and boxers off. Normally, he would neatly fold them or have her do it for him, but tonight, he kicked them aside, a sure sign that he was losing his control.

He held his big dick in one hand and her head in the other. His fingers tangled in her hair and he pulled slightly, barely a little sting. The sawhorse was perfectly adjusted to place her mouth right where he wanted it. "Get me hard. Your Master wants to fuck his sub."

She almost laughed. He was so hard he could pound nails. She doubted the enormous cock in front of her could get any harder, but she didn't question him. No, she simply opened her mouth and let him push his way in. He didn't require anything active from her when he was in this state. He merely wanted her compliance, and she gave it to him. He thrust himself in and out of her willing mouth.

His cock thrust forward as his hands pulled her head in. "That's my good sub. Open wide for your Master. Your Master is going to fuck your mouth, then he's going to take that hot ass of yours and give you a reaming you won't forget."

She let his deep voice wash over her as he promised all manner of nasty things. The dirty talk had always been a part of their play, and hearing Cal whisper what he intended to do to her got her even hotter. Closing her eyes, she reveled in the feel of him. Her whole body was primed for sensation. She loved the salty taste of his cock, the silky steel feel of his thrusting dick as he worked his way in inch by inch until his balls hit her chin. He smelled like arousal and soap from a shower. He was Callum, her lover, her Master, and everything about him made her think of home.

Cal pulled out of her mouth. He was shaking a little, and he wiped away a tear she hadn't known she'd shed. He got down on one knee and kissed her forehead. "I missed you."

Emotion swelled as she let the experience wash over her. She'd missed him so much. She had no idea where they went from here, if they went anywhere at all. She only knew that, for these moments, she was his again.

Cal got back up, tossed off his shirt, and he was magnificently naked. She watched as he walked around to her naked backside. The crowd was bigger than before. Gaby could plainly see the scene was having an effect on some of the men.

"Eyes on me and only me," Cal growled, smacking her ass.

She obediently looked straight on in the mirror, watching her Master. His cock jutted up, almost reaching his navel. The gorgeous purple head was filled with blood, and a drop of pearly arousal wept from his slit. He reached over to the table where the toys were kept. Gaby sighed as he wrapped an elastic strap around her hips and through her thighs. He carefully placed the butterfly directly over her clit. It hummed when he turned it on, and the vibrator started her on a slow build toward climax.

"If you come before I allow it, I'll get out the single tail, Gabrielle."

She bit her lip. It would be hard. The vibrator was doing all sorts of things to her clit. While she let the sensation play across her body, Cal was busy. It wasn't more than a few seconds before he spread the cheeks of her ass and pulled out the plug. She moaned as her asshole fought to keep that little piece of plastic. Cal set the plug to the side and started to work warm lube into her.

She gasped as he forced a finger in. He rimmed her, eliciting a groan as all of those nerves so long forgotten came roaring back to life. She forgot about the people watching, forgot about the trouble with Cal. Hell, she forgot about the last ten months. All that mattered was him and the pleasure he gave her.

"Push back." Cal sounded guttural.

Something far bigger than his finger was seeking entrance. His cock was larger than the plug, and she hissed at the pressure. The butterfly went up a notch. Gaby had to concentrate on pushing back against Cal's cock. She went on her tiptoes and angled her hips up. It burned as he began to thrust in, stretching her to take him. She was caught between the heat filling her ass and the wild pleasure spreading across her clitoris.

"Oh, you feel so fucking good." Cal tunneled his way in ruthlessly. He pushed past the ring of her anus and seated his cock in her tight ass. For a moment, she wondered if he was going to split her in two, he was so fucking big. She could feel his balls caress the cheeks of her ass. He pulled almost all the way out and greedily shoved back in. Every nerve in her backside sang as his cock dragged along them. In and out. In and out.

Cal fucked her with a steady rhythm. His hands tightened on her waist, holding her steady for the thorough reaming he'd promised. She had to bite her lip to keep from coming. It was all building. The riotous sensation in her ass combined with the sweet hum on her clit was proving too much for her.

Cal picked up the pace, his cock thrusting hard now. "I'm not going to last. It's been too long. You need to come for me. Come for your Master."

The butterfly hit the perfect spot. Cal's cock rubbed just the right place, and Gaby sobbed as she came. She forced her eyes open, not wanting to miss the sight of Cal taking his pleasure. She loved the way his dark head fell back when he gave over. His entire body stiffened as the orgasm hit. He breathed out, and his gorgeous face contorted with the sweetest agony imaginable. His hands tightened on her hips. He thrust into her one last time as she felt the hot wash of his release flood her ass.

A great sense of peace washed over her when Cal let his body fall forward across hers. She felt his lips on the back of her neck, worshipping the soft skin there. His cock came out of her ass, and he flicked off the butterfly. It wouldn't take long before Cal was ready to go again. He'd never had a problem with performance. He would want to fuck her over and over again. He would take her all night long.

Cal's hands slid up her torso and under her shirt. "I want you naked, Gabrielle. I want to play with those pretty nipples."

"Red."

Her whole world seemed to stop. It all crashed down as she said the one word she'd never uttered to him before.

"Red."

Callum seemed stunned, but immediately got off her, stepping back almost as if she was on fire.

"Gabrielle?" There was a wealth of hurt in the question.

"I said red." She forced the words out of her mouth. Tears stung her eyes. She couldn't do it. She couldn't let him see her. He'd always loved her breasts. He'd taken such pride in showing her off. How could she ever show him what had happened? She wanted to run, but the bindings were tight. Now she realized everyone was watching this, too. The crowd had grown. Everyone could see her and the sad end of the scene playing out like entertainment.

His hand touched her skin. "Gabrielle, please."

"I'm sorry." James stepped up. "She said her safe word. I need you to move away from her."

In the mirror, she could see through her tears that Cal was pale. His hands shook as he managed to get his slacks on.

"Take care of her." Cal's voice was low and tense. "She won't let me."

James pulled the bindings off her wrists. He had a robe in his hand and wrapped it around her. Gaby sat down in the middle of the dungeon, put her head in her hands, and cried.

Chapter Five

Cal let his head rest against the cool glass of the windowpane. He stared out at the sapphire blue of the sea, but he didn't really see it. Though it was seven in the morning, he reached out and brought a glass to his lips, the Scotch burning its way down his throat. He shook his head. It didn't matter how much he drank. It wouldn't erase the memory of Gabrielle pushing him away.

Red. That one word would haunt him the rest of his life.

He was tired, so fucking tired. He was tired of longing for Gabrielle. He was tired of hiding behind Cassie's memory. He was tired of everything.

Cal put down the Scotch. It wouldn't really help, anyway. He'd done so much damage that Gabrielle no longer trusted him. He had no illusions as to why she'd used her safe word. She truly believed he would push her away when he saw the scars on her body. She couldn't think very much of him if she believed him to be that shallow.

He couldn't blame her. He'd never opened himself to her. He'd taken all her softness and offered very little in return.

Cal slapped at the window. She deserved better. She deserved a man who could give her everything, a man who knew how to love, a man who hadn't fucked up everything. Cal wondered how many lives he would ruin before he was done. He closed his eyes, and he could see Cassie, so young. He could still see her devastated body on the gurney in the emergency room before they wheeled her into the OR.

He'd only just managed to make it there. She'd been dazed with pain and drugs, and her last moments hadn't been ones of peace.

She wouldn't have died if he'd done his job.

His failures weighed heavily on him. He hadn't been there, but he could still hear Gaby crying for him when she came out of her surgery. He'd cared for two women in his life, and he'd so deeply failed them both that he knew he would never try again. He would give Gabrielle what he could and get out of her life.

But he owed her an explanation.

Cal pushed away from the window and crossed to the closet. He tossed his suitcase on the bed and picked up the phone. It wasn't more than a second before an efficient desk clerk answered.

He listened to her greeting and got to his point. "Yes. I'm in the Angelina Suite. I'm leaving today. I need a boat to pick me up. Thank you."

Cal packed, trying not to think about the fact that this would be the last time he saw Gabrielle. The years spread out before him, and he knew how they would go. He would be alone. He deserved it. He would listen every time Heather or Greg spoke, hoping to hear any brief mention of her. Gabrielle, herself, would move on eventually. She would find someone who could love her with a free heart. She would be the sunshine in her husband's life. She would give him children and have a happy life. She would have everything she deserved, and if that man ever stepped out of line, Cal would kill him.

When his bags were packed and he'd made sure there would be no trace of him left, Cal made another call, this one to a lawyer. When he was sure he'd done everything he needed to, Cal showered, dressed, and went to find Gabrielle.

She was in her office, as he thought she would be.

"Could you please tell Ms. Sullivan I would like to speak with her?" Cal was excruciatingly polite to Gaby's administrative assistant.

She put in the call. After a moment, she nodded. "You can go in."

"Thank you. And, Jackie, you'll be getting several emails from a law firm in Freeport. Please make sure they're printed out, copied, and properly filed." Callum took a deep breath and walked into Gabrielle's office.

She was sitting at her desk, but looked up when the door opened.

She seemed fragile in the morning light. A sense of guilt settled in Cal's heart. He'd brought that pale, tired look to her face. She'd been getting better, according to Cody. Now she was sad again because of him.

"Cal," she started.

He stopped her, putting a hand up. "Don't, sweetheart. I just came by to say good-bye."

She huffed, and a flush raced across her skin. "All right. Good-bye, Cal."

She looked back down at her laptop, dismissing him.

The Dom in him wanted to snarl at her and force her to look at him. He pushed the impulse down. He wasn't going to leave until she understood. She needed to know that what had gone wrong between them was a flaw in him, not her. He sank down in the chair across from her desk.

"I married Cassie when we were very young. I explained that to you, but I can't express her youth in mere age. Cassie was a child, really."

"You were eighteen too, Cal." She seemed almost angry that she'd said it. Her pretty mouth was a stubborn line.

"Yes, now I can see what a child I was. At the time, I wanted Cassandra because she was lovely and she needed me. She needed me so much. I grew up very wealthy. I was an only child, as though my parents knew they had some kind of duty to all that money. They had me and then promptly went back to their jet-setting lives, leaving me alone with nannies and servants. My parents barely remembered they had a child. They spent all their time at parties and mingling with the right people. The only time I was paraded out was to show their friends how perfect I was. Cassie was the first person to need me. I felt like a man when she looked to me for strength. Her father was our gardener. We were eight when we met. She became my friend, and looking back now, I became her everything. It was quite easy to go from friendship to something more as we grew older. I got her pregnant the month we finished high school."

She gasped, her eyes widening and softening at the news. "I never knew."

He sent her a small smile. "Of course, I never told you."

He didn't miss the way her hands clenched together. She had guessed how the story went. "How did the child die?"

"He was stillborn." Cal's throat felt too tight as he pushed the words out. "She was in her eighth month when the doctor couldn't find a heartbeat anymore. It broke something in Cassie. She'd always preferred to have me make the decisions, but after we lost our son, she completely withdrew from the world."

"Heather told me she seemed a bit like a ghost."

It was an apt analogy. When he thought of Cassie now, she seemed ethereal and insubstantial compared to Gabrielle's solid strength. "I suppose she was. We fell into a pattern after that. I went to school, went to work, and she stayed home. She would keep the house fairly clean, but only if I instructed her to. She would get up and get dressed, but only if I laid her clothes out and told her to."

"She was depressed."

"I realize that now." Another mistake he'd made. Another way he'd failed. "Then, I was very young and on my own for the first time. It took everything I had to keep my head above water. I came into my trust fund at twenty-one, and that helped enormously. While I was in law school, I was able to move us to a better part of town and hire a maid. Greg was an old friend. We reconnected in law school, and he introduced Cassie and me to the scene. Strangely, the club was one of the only places where Cassie came to life. Our sex life improved significantly when we discovered D/s. Cassie seemed more comfortable and, after a while, started calling me Master. She never called me anything else when we weren't in the vanilla world."

Gabrielle was very quiet for a moment, as though she needed time to properly digest the history he spilled out for her. "Why didn't you have kids?"

He laughed, but there was no humor behind it. "Oh, we tried. Cassie was obsessed with it. She couldn't get pregnant after that first time. The doctor said it was a miracle she'd gotten pregnant at all. I offered to adopt, but she didn't want to. After a while, I was happy we didn't. I would have had to hire a nanny. Cassie retreated. She rarely did anything on her own. I had to tell her what and when to eat. When I tried to take her to a psychologist, she'd cry and tell me I didn't love her."

Gabrielle's hazel eyes bored through him. "Cal, that is no way to live."

"I know, but I lived that way for years. I promised to love her. I promised to take care of her. On the night she died, I told her I wanted a divorce."

Her eyes watered, and she reached out to him. "Oh, Callum, you are not responsible for her death. You can't possibly think that."

She was far too forgiving, his Gabrielle. He shook his head. "She hadn't driven in years. She got into the car, and an hour later, I got the call from the hospital. I rushed there, and she was dying. She begged me. She begged me not to leave her. She made me promise I wouldn't love anyone but her. I told her I wouldn't. When she died, I promised myself I wouldn't get involved with another slave. I wouldn't have another woman dependent on me, and what did I do? I immediately found you."

"Not exactly immediately. It was a year later." Her voice was soft now, soothing. "You need to be in control. It's part of who you are. But, Cal, she had no right to ask that of you. If she loved you at all, she would want you to be happy."

He sighed. He should have known her tender heart wouldn't understand. "Have you listened to anything I've said? I helped her become dependent on me and then couldn't stand the fact that she was. I didn't even truly want the divorce. I was using it as a way to force her to see a counselor. I couldn't give her what she needed. I tried, but I didn't. I didn't give you what you needed, either."

She started to protest, but he held a hand up. "I allowed myself to take you for granted. You were right. I wanted a convenient body in my bed and a woman who didn't depend on me for everything. Damn it, in a lot of ways I treated you the opposite of Cassie. I would never have left her alone the way I did you. I would never have given her work from my office. I would never, ever have broken a date with her for work."

"You didn't want to be in a relationship like that again. But our relationship didn't work like that. I remember the day after I moved in. You laid out clothes for me." Even years later, there was accusation in her voice, though it was softened with a fond smile.

Cal felt a wide grin spread across his face as the memory warmed

102

him. God, at least he would have his memories of her. "I remember that you told me if I liked the clothes that much, I could wear them."

"I got a spanking, but you didn't lay them out again."

Looking back now, he could see that it had been everything he could have wanted. If he'd only been brave enough to really reach out to her, maybe things would have been different. He wouldn't have lost her trust. "Gabrielle, I think you're beautiful. I'll always think you're beautiful. Trust me. Show me."

Her hands crossed her chest, and she shook her head. "I can't."

He took a deep breath. He hadn't meant to make the plea. He had meant to say good-bye. Now it looked like it was time to do just that. "All right. I'm leaving on the noon boat. I won't bother you again. If you ever need anything, you know where I am."

His hand was on the door when her soft voice called to him.

"Thank you, Cal, for explaining why you couldn't love me."

He felt his breath hitch. "Gabrielle, I loved you the minute I saw you. I love you so much, my heart aches with it. It was one more vow I broke."

He heard her start to cry as he closed the door. He hoped it was the very last time she had to cry over him.

He nodded briefly to the admin and made his way out of the office.

"Is that it, then?"

Cody Linwood stood just outside the door. It was the last thing he needed. He wanted to be alone. He wanted to mourn her. "I have a boat to make, if you don't mind."

Linwood sighed and fell into step. "You're leaving?"

"You don't understand, and it really isn't any of your business."

Cody laughed, a sharp sound. "Let's see if I've got it. You took Gaby to the dungeon, spanked her ass, fucked her ass, and then she used her safe word. You think she doesn't trust you. She thinks you don't love her. You're both dumbasses. Now, you're going to leave and hope she has a happy life, and she's going to let you because she's scared you won't ever love her."

Cal stopped in the middle of the hall. He leaned over the smaller man and growled slightly. "You don't know anything. I told her I loved her."

Cody took a step forward, not giving in an inch to Cal's threat. "And she should believe you, why?"

"I have never lied to Gabrielle. I might have lied to myself, but never to her. It wasn't until she left that I truly understood how much I love her and how long I've loved her. It's simply too late."

"Those are all fine words, Callum, but have you backed them up?"

Cal wanted to punch the kid. "What do you want me to do? Should I go in there and force a ring on her finger? I made her play a role for years. I won't force her into anything else. She needs to be in control now."

Cody brightened. "See, you can learn."

"What are you talking about now?"

"There's only one way to win this fight, Callum. I know Gaby still loves you, but she's afraid. She's afraid you'll reject her. You have to show her you're willing to change. The Dom in you is going to have to surrender."

"What do you mean?" Cal's brain was working, the idea tickling at the edges of his consciousness.

"You required her submission. She gave it to you. It was the way she proved she loved and trusted you. Do you love her? Do you trust her?"

Cal stopped. Could it work? Could he actually do that? Hell, yes, he could. If it would give Gabrielle a minute's peace, he could do anything. "How good are you with knots?"

"As it happens, I'm quite good."

Chapter Six

Gaby stared at the computer in front of her, but all she could see was Cal's face. He'd looked incredibly sincere when he'd turned and told her he'd always loved her. He'd looked like a man who'd just figured something important out and knew the revelation had come too late.

And it *was* too late. Wasn't it? She couldn't go back to the way things were. Cal couldn't change.

Except he'd left his work behind to pursue her. Never once had he done that before. Work was everything to him. And he'd explained his past with Cassie. The past had been off limits. A no-go zone.

And he'd tried to get her to marry him and told her he loved her. All things he'd sworn he wouldn't do.

How could he possibly blame himself for Cassie's death? He'd been a child when they married. Their marriage had been marked with tragedy. Losing a child the way they had, it broke many marriages. He had to be able to see that it wasn't his fault. Cassie had retreated, and Cal had taken control. Gaby had no doubt that if Cassie hadn't gotten into a car that night, she would have sought help before letting Cal leave her. Cassie's dying wish had been one of a desperate woman. He couldn't be held to it.

Her heart ached at the thought of Cal thinking he was faithless when he was simply human. He deserved the chance to love again, to make another life.

To stand beside the woman he loved and help her through the

worst of all times.

In sickness and in health. They hadn't been married, hadn't made vows, but she knew what she would have done if it had been him.

Had she taken his rights away because she'd wanted to spare him pain or because she'd been afraid?

Or had there been something more?

"Gaby?"

Gaby looked up to see her admin nervously poking her head in the door.

"I didn't want to disturb you, but we got these contracts in and I thought you should see them."

She waved her admin off. She couldn't think about work right now. "Call Cody. Have him take a look. I think I'm going to take the rest of the day off."

She would go to the beach and sit. She would think about what she'd done and honestly figure out the whys. It seemed simple in the moment, but nothing about a real relationship was simple. Love was complex and difficult. It was about more than three little words. It was about actions. His. Hers.

Jackie vigorously shook her head. "No. It's about you. That man who was in here, he signed over his part of the resort to you. You now own twenty-five percent of this place."

What? The world seemed to still as she tried to process. He'd done that for her? He'd given up the one piece on the board he could hold over her head?

Maybe he was done and he didn't want to bother anymore.

God, where had that cynicism come from? It wasn't her and she had to stop putting it on him. Yes, he'd said things that were horrible, but then she looked at what he'd actually done.

What if this was a simple gift from a broken, loving Master? From a Master who couldn't perform his duties, who couldn't serve his purpose anymore? He could give her something to protect her. He could give her something to lift her up.

Tears pooled in her eyes. What was she doing? Was she really going to let him walk out because she was afraid? And what exactly was she afraid of? That Cal would take one look at her and reject her because she had some scars?

Jackie placed the papers on her desk and then seemed to understand she needed to be alone. The door closed, and she looked down at what Callum had given her. He'd given her what a true Dom should. He'd given her what she needed—control. Cal thought she needed this place and to be in control of her future. She'd told him as much.

But what she hadn't said was that she really needed him.

Letting her head fall into her hands, she wept. She wept for what she'd lost. She wouldn't breastfeed her children. She wouldn't feel Cal's lips tug on her nipples again. She'd lost her mother at the age of forty-two to the same disease that ravaged her body. She cried for that. She cried because she should have been brave enough to tell Callum what she needed. She should have stayed and fought with everything she had.

After a long while, she looked up at the clock. It was late morning. She shot out of her chair. Almost noon. She would miss his boat. She left the papers on her desk and ran out of the office, her legs sprinting. She ran past the lobby and out toward the dock just in time to see the boat headed for Freeport take off.

Too late.

Ten minutes later, she made her way back into the resort and headed for her room. She'd tried, but they wouldn't turn the boat back. She'd thought briefly about swimming but figured that only worked in the movies. She would have to suck it up and take the next boat out. She would get on a plane and fly to Fort Worth. She wasn't going to let him get away from her again. She would find him and tell him.

I love you, too. I loved you from the moment I saw you. I knew you. I won't ever leave you again.

Resolute, she made her way to her suite. She would pack and be ready for the next ferry out.

She stopped, and her mouth dropped open at the scene that greeted her when she entered her bedroom with every intention of packing her belongings. There was a naked man bound on her bed. His muscular body was tied to the headboard and footboard. He looked delicious spread out on her sheets, his tanned skin contrasting with the stark white of her bedding. He was laid out, a feast for her delectation.

"Cal? You didn't leave?" She gasped the question, almost not believing her eyes.

His head came up. For the first time in their relationship, she found Cal was hesitant, nervous even. His gorgeous face with his perfectly square jaw was open to her. His dark eyes took her in, and he licked his lips with a nervous swipe of his tongue.

"I know I said I would, but Gabrielle, I have to try everything. I want to be with you. I couldn't leave until I was sure I'd done everything I could to make it all up to you." He inclined his head to the table by the bed. "There's a gag over there if you want it. I thought it might be uncomfortable, so I had Cody leave it out."

She stared. She found herself quite unable to move. "Cody did this?"

"Well, pet, I am very talented when it comes to bondage, but I'm afraid I am not capable of tying myself up."

"And he left you?" A Dom never left a bound sub alone. Anything could happen.

A flush crept across Cal's skin. "He fought me on that. My lovely pet, I am willing to do many things to win you back. Sitting here naked with your gay nurse reading the latest *Us Weekly* is not one of them. I need to maintain some semblance of dignity."

He was spread eagle across her fluffy white comforter, next to a tray of sex toys. She felt a smile cross her face. If he had any dignity left, she wasn't sure where it was. But she *was* sure of one thing. "You love me."

All hesitancy left his face. He turned very serious. "I love you, Gabrielle. I don't know how good I am at it, though. It might not be worth much."

A slow happiness built in her veins. Her big, strong Dom was submitting to her. It was more than she would have imagined Cal could give. This went against his very nature, and yet he had done it for her. In her dreams, she'd imagined him on one knee telling her how much she meant to him. But this was Callum. This was more romantic than a thousand roses. "Hush, now, sub. I'll tell you when you can talk."

His eyes flared, and it looked like he was going to tell her what she could do with her command. She gave him a moment, and his mouth closed.

"Very good, sub." Starting at his toes, she let her fingers trail up the firm muscles of his leg. The skin was smooth, and the dark hair on it felt crisp under her hand. "You're quite a pretty submissive. I wonder what I should do with you. Oh, my, this is a lovely bounty you have here."

She stared down at his cock. It swelled before her eyes. It had gotten hard the minute she touched him, but now it was reaching the epic proportions she was used to. She cupped his balls, and a pearly drop wept from the tip of his erection. She rolled his balls gently in the palm of her hand. A fine bead of sweat broke out on his forehead.

Gaby grinned. She knew exactly what he was feeling. He wanted to toss her on the bed, force her legs apart, and shove that big dick as far into her pussy as it would go. He wanted to fuck her so hard she would never forget who her Master was. Unfortunately, this was her show, and she planned to play it up before she ceded control again for good.

She looked over at the toys on the table. A bounty of pleasures and she was the Mistress of them all. Actually, she could get used to this. Cody had done a wonderful job. He'd left her with many toys to use on a poor bound submissive. There was a nice-sized vibrator and something else that caught her eye—a plastic plug. She was smiling as she picked up the vibe. She turned it on and sank to the bed next to Cal. He moaned when she used the vibrating cock as a wand, rubbing it over his own weeping cock. Tied up as he was, Cal could do nothing except twist and writhe.

"That's an impressive array of toys, my sub." She let the vibe rub all along his skin. Cal's head fell back. His eyes closed as a low moan rumbled from his chest. He was obviously drowning in sensation, and she suddenly understood why he loved to torture her. He was beautiful like this. Every muscle in his body was tense, his face tight. When he looked back up at her, his eyes were glazed with passion. She was giving this to him. It made her feel powerful, but there was also a sweet warmth to it. "Do you like this, sub?"

His head came up. There was a fire in his eyes as he pulled at his restraints. He would never be able to completely submit. He would be a good boy for now, but there would be hell to pay later. Her pussy wept at the thought of Cal's revenge. "You're going to kill me, Gabrielle."

"Gabrielle?" She mimicked Cal's arrogant Dom tone.

A little grin crossed his face. "Mistress."

"Better." His cock was straining. The vein that ran on the underside was pulsing. He was getting close, and that just wouldn't do. She pulled the vibrator away. Her sweet, arrogant sub groaned in frustration. "Not yet, sub."

She picked up another toy. It was a very flexible toy that tapered on one end and on the other end had a bulbous head to keep it locked inside the wearer. She knew it well. "A butt plug, Cal? Seriously? You want to walk around with a plug up your ass?"

"No, Gabrielle...Mistress." He seemed flustered. His hips pumped up as though his cock longed for the touch of the vibe again. "I think it sounds perfectly dreadful, but I'm willing to take it if it pleases you."

She straddled him, rubbing her core against his straining cock. Even through the fabric of her shorts, she could feel how hard he was. She rubbed her clit along his dick and sighed at the sensation. She leaned forward and shook that little piece of plastic in his face. She came out of her mistress role for a moment. "This is tiny, Cal. This is half the size of what you lovingly shove up my ass on a regular basis."

His voice came out in breathless pants. "That is exactly the size I started you on, pet. I worked you up to a larger size so you could gradually accommodate this."

He pushed up against her, leaving no doubt as to what he meant.

"You know this is very good therapy for us. I'm beginning to understand why you love this. You love being able to watch me, to know you're the one making me moan and groan and that I wouldn't do it for anyone else."

His eyes flared. "Then know that I'm beginning to understand you, too. You love this because you trust me like no one else. Because no one on earth makes you feel as vulnerable as I can and as powerful, too."

"Then we, my love, are making some serious headway because I never thought we could do this, could understand each other on this level. I thank you for this gift." She tossed the plug on the tray. She wasn't about to use it on him, but there was something he might enjoy. She leaned across him and picked up the lube. She coated her hands and then kneeled between his bound legs. She had read about this, but this was the first time she was in a position to try it. She winked at him as she leaned over and very deliberately licked from the base of his cock to the head. Cal's breath came out as a long hiss.

"Relax, love."

She leaned forward and took the head of Cal's cock in her mouth, teasing it lightly. While she ran her tongue all along the head, Gaby very gently parted the muscled cheeks of his ass. She licked the slit of his cock, sucking lightly to draw out the salty essence. While Cal moaned and strained, she started to work her middle finger into Cal's tight asshole.

"Gabrielle!"

She looked up as Cal squirmed. She remembered all the times they had played Master and slave games. She knew exactly what to say to him. "You hold still. This is my plaything to do with as I like. Your cock is mine. Your ass is mine, too. If I want to fuck your ass with my fingers, then I will. Unless you want to use your safe word. Just say 'red,' and I'll stop."

His face turned very stubborn, his sensual lips forming a flat line. He stopped moving, and his head found the pillow again. He seemed to try to relax. She licked his cock like a lollipop. Her tongue curled around the ridge where the head met the thick stalk of his dick. All the while, she teased her finger into his tight hole. His anus resisted, trying to push her out. She rimmed the rigid hole with her well-lubed finger and pressed in. Cal groaned when she finally pushed past his initial resistance and sank in. She sucked at her treat and twisted her finger deep inside his ass.

It was time to give her Master the ride of his life.

* * * *

Cal strained against the ropes. Cody had been right about his skill with the bondage arts. The restraints were perfectly tied to hold him but keep the circulation flowing. It was too perfect. He wished the nurse had proven a bit looser in his habits. Then he could pull his hands out and do what he wanted. He could take Gabrielle, throw her on her hands and knees, and fuck her like the animal he felt like. He needed her on a primal level. He'd been insane with the need to get inside her since she walked in the door and he'd realized she wasn't walking back out.

But then, no. Like she'd said, they needed this. They needed to understand each other, and this exercise put him in the position to do exactly that. He hoped he looked down at her like she was staring at him. When she was bound for his pleasure, he prayed he looked at her with the same wonder and lust and love she'd shown him. He felt frustrated and cherished and adored.

It was a gift to see things through her eyes.

Her mouth closed over his cock and sucked him deep. His cock was enveloped in the heat of her. Just as he adjusted to the feel of her sucking around him, she twisted the finger she'd shoved up his ass. It burned, and then she found some spot deep inside of him that made him twist, trying to get her to hit it again.

Prostate. Cal found the word he was looking for. It helped keep him from exploding in her mouth. His balls felt like they were about to explode. He couldn't, wouldn't come until she'd given him permission. He tried to concentrate on the foreign sensation.

He'd been shocked when she'd first done it. He wanted to protest, but a part of him was intrigued, too. He'd only explored a part of his sexuality. His role had been very rigid up until now, but she was opening it up for him with every pass of that curious finger of hers. That little finger fucked in and out of his anus. She pressed deep and then dragged slowly back out. He shuddered as nerves he'd never known he had came roaring to life. There was so much more he and Gabrielle had to explore if he would open himself to it.

She swirled his cock in her mouth as she massaged a second finger deep into his ass. He nearly cried out. His whole body was ready to detonate, but he knew the game. She was going to torture him, and he was going to take it. She wasn't going to make it easy on him. She dragged her fingers over the nub of his prostate, and he thought he was going to scream. Between the softness of her mouth and the biting edge of her finger, he was losing the battle to not come.

Cal watched her head move up and down on his cock. Over and over again, she sucked him down. His cock was so hard it was a deep purple as it sank into her mouth. She opened as wide as she could when she took him to that soft place in the back of her throat, but she was still small. He could feel the edge of her teeth lightly scraping as he bucked up into her. She paused above him, giving him a wicked smile.

"Do you want to come, sub?"

"Please, Mistress." He was past caring what she called him. If he'd been able, he would have pleaded on his hands and knees. He just wanted to release the tension. He wanted to flood her mouth and watch her drink him down.

A brilliant smile crossed her beautiful face. "Then come for me, Callum."

Her mouth sucked him down with sexy greed. He watched his cock disappear, felt her tongue roll. He hissed as she rubbed the nub of his prostate, and he couldn't hold back. His balls drew up, and he shot off like a rocket. He sighed and writhed as every bit of semen he had flowed from his cock into her sweet mouth. She pulled her finger out and concentrated on licking him clean. He wanted so badly to tangle his hands in her hair, to whisper how much she pleased him.

Instead, she gave his softening cock one last lick and then moved up his prone body. She loomed over him, a dreamy look on her face. She seemed utterly satisfied, and he knew he'd given her something special.

He'd given them something special—the chance to see life, to see their love through each other's eyes. He'd thought this was a desperate play to get her back, but it proved to be what he needed to see her, really see her as the beautiful partner she was to him. They didn't need rigid rules. They could move fluidly, each strengthening the other because they had been born to lift each other up.

His sub. His wife. The other half of his soul.

"Thank you, sub." She leaned down and pressed her mouth to his. The kiss was brief and sweet. She reached up and began pulling at his bindings. "Now, I would like my sweet Master back."

He felt satiated, but far from satisfied. When she'd undone his bindings, he rolled on top of her, crushing her small form beneath his own. He pulled her into his arms, kissing her soundly. Her mouth opened under his. He tangled his tongue with hers, tasting his own salty flavor.

"I love you, Gabrielle. Can you forgive me?" He looked down into her serious gray-green eyes. She slowly pushed up against him, her hands small on his chest. Cal took his weight off her. He rolled onto his back as she got up off the bed. Her face was solemn, and his heart skipped a beat as her fingers undid the top button of her shirt.

He held his breath. He wasn't worried about what he would see. He knew exactly what she'd gone through on a surgical level. He'd studied up on the protocols for dealing with a cancer like hers and understood what had happened. But he knew how hard it was for her to do this and gave it all the weight it deserved.

Slowly, she pulled the shirt off. She was wearing a pale pink bra beneath it. He could see her hands shaking as she reached around to undo the clasp. His first instinct was to do it for her, but he held back. His Gabrielle was very strong. She needed to do this for herself. The bra slipped from her hands, and Cal smiled.

"Oh, baby, you're beautiful." He meant it. There were scars. They began under her armpits and curved around her chest. Though the plastic surgeon had been very skilled, there was no question her chest had suffered a horrible trauma. Livid, raised lines crossed her body, and where her nipples used to be, there was only a flat patch of brownish skin. To Cal, they were lovely. It meant she was alive. They would stand on her body, forever a testament to her will to survive.

Cal sat up on the side of the bed. He drew her in between his legs. She was petite, so his head was in the perfect position to play with her breasts. He traced each puckered scar with his fingers, learning the feel of them. He let his hand find her "nipples." They were really just circles of a rosy brown color. They didn't react to touch or tighten when the air got cool. He couldn't clamp them or pinch them between his thumb and forefinger. Those nipples were nothing more than a simple tattoo, and yet they seemed like a magnificent work of art. He kissed them tenderly.

"Cal, I can't feel it." She sounded disappointed and a bit apologetic.

"But I can." She needed to understand he would still find pleasure in her breasts because they were a part of her. Every part and piece of her was a pleasure to him, a gift.

She sighed, and her hands found his hair. He kissed along one and then the other breast, pushed them up so he could lay kisses along the scars underneath. He reveled in the warmth of her skin and the smell of her body.

He looked up at her, one hand between her breasts. "This has always been my favorite part of you, Gabrielle. That is never going to change."

She smiled at him with watery eyes. "Thank you, but it's okay. I know how different they are."

"There's no difference at all." He kissed the flesh in the middle of her chest. "I was talking about your heart, Gabrielle."

His arms wound around her and pulled her down into his embrace. He flipped her underneath his body and made a place for himself at her core. His cock was already hard again. He would never get used to how much he wanted her. He kissed her like he'd wanted to for almost a year. His tongue mated with hers wildly, showing her what he wanted to do. He fought to pull her shorts down and rid her of the panties he fully intended to burn once their relationship was on a proper footing. He tossed them off the bed. There was no chance that she would need clothes again this day. He came up for air. There was one thing they needed to get straight.

"This does mean you'll marry me, right?"

There was a distinctly sly smile on her face. "I don't recall being asked. I recall a very arrogant man telling me I would marry him and follow him back to Fort Worth. The only trouble with that is now I seem to have come into a little property."

He groaned. He'd made a monster. "We'll stay here as long as you like, but I'll need to set up an office. Greg is my biggest client. I can do most of his work from here."

She looked very surprised. "Cal, I was joking. I'll come back."

"I think you need to be here for a while. It's peaceful. Do you love it here?" He smoothed back her hair, and the glow in her face answered his question.

She nodded. "But not more than I love you."

115

"Then, Gabrielle Sullivan, will you marry me?" He grinned down at her. Finally, she was where she belonged, beneath him, grounding him. "You know I don't like to hear no from my pretty little sub."

She moved restlessly against him. He could feel how wet she was. He slid his cock all over her pussy, gliding easily around the juicy flesh. "Yes, Callum."

He pushed her legs apart and slammed home. This was what he missed. He shoved his cock in until his balls slapped at her ass and held himself there. Her pussy clenched around him, a tight vise on his flesh. Her hands dug into his ass. He slipped his hand in between them and toyed with her clit. "Do you want to come, my sub?"

"Oh, yes, Cal."

He pinched down firmly, making her writhe around him. "What do you call me?"

"Master. Yes, Master."

He started thrusting into his gorgeous submissive. He reared back and slammed home. He reveled in their connection. "Master in the bedroom, Gabrielle. Husband everywhere else. Partners always."

Her face flushed. Her arms wrapped around his shoulders, and her ankles locked at his waist. He stroked her clit again, and she came. He felt every little muscle in her cunt start to milk his cock. It was too delicious to deny. He thrust in one last time and gave over. She gasped and whimpered as he came inside her. When he was completely drained, he fell on her, withholding none of his weight.

"Cal." She sounded a little panicked. "Oh, Cal, I'm not on anything. I'm not on any birth control."

He hugged her tightly to him. Now it was his turn to be brave. "I know. I want to have a family with you. Just understand when I'm unsettled."

Her smile was brilliant. "I'll be with you. I'll be with you all the way."

He rolled her on the bed. She wouldn't leave again. If she did, he would be right there, running after her. "Of that I have no doubt."

Cal kissed his bride-to-be and started the process all over again.

Author's Note

I'm often asked by generous readers how they can help get the word out about a book they enjoyed. There are so many ways to help an author you like. Leave a review. If your e-reader allows you to lend a book to a friend, please share it. Go to Goodreads and connect with others. Recommend the books you love because stories are meant to be shared. Thank you so much for reading this book and for supporting all the authors you love!

Sign up for Lexi Blake's newsletter
and be entered to win a $25 gift certificate
to the bookseller of your choice.

Join us for news, fun, and exclusive content
including free short stories.

There's a new contest every month!

Click here to subscribe.

Nobody Does It Better
Masters and Mercenaries 15
By Lexi Blake
Coming February 20, 2018
Click here to pre-order

A spy who specializes in seduction

Kayla Summers was an elite CIA double agent, working inside China's deadly MSS. Now, she works for McKay-Taggart London, but the Agency isn't quite done with her. Spy master Ezra Fain needs her help on a mission that would send her into Hollywood's glamorous and dangerous party scene. Intrigued by the mission and the movie star hunk she will be shadowing, she eagerly agrees. When she finds herself in his bed, she realizes she's not only risking her life, but her heart.

A leading man who doesn't do romance

Joshua Hunt is a legend of the silver screen. As Hollywood's highest paid actor, he's the man everyone wants to be, or be with, but something is missing. After being betrayed more than once, the only romance Josh believes in anymore is on the pages of his scripts. He keeps his relationships transactional, and that's how he likes it, until he meets his new bodyguard. She was supposed to keep him safe, and satisfied when necessary, but now he's realizing he may never be able to get enough of her.

An ending neither could have expected

Protecting Joshua started off as a mission, until it suddenly felt like her calling. When the true reason the CIA wanted her for this assignment is revealed, Kayla will have to choose between serving her country or saving the love of her life.

* * * *

"Kayla?"

Her eyes came up, a flash of recognition there. "Yes?"

"Are you going to sign the contract or do you have more questions?"

She picked up the pen sitting on top of the contracts that would bind the two of them together for the next six months. They would reevaluate the relationship at that point in time, but for the next six months, she was his. His bodyguard. His submissive.

Bought and properly paid for. He would take care of her and she would give him what he needed.

She signed with a flourish and sat back, a gleam of curiosity in her eyes.

He was curious, too, and there was zero reason to not satisfy their curiosity. Hard and soft limits had been gone over. They would find their communication style as they went along. But first she should understand that he was in control.

"Come sit on my lap."

She didn't hesitate. She stood and turned, shifting so she could maneuver her way onto his lap.

Her weight came down on him and he wrapped an arm around her waist. Damn but she made him feel big. He'd seen her take out a man twice her size, but sitting here in his lap she felt small and vulnerable, and fuck him but that did it for him.

He slid a hand along her knee, letting himself indulge in the silky smooth feel of her skin against his palm. "Did you do as I asked?"

He was well aware his voice had gone husky, deeper than normal.

"Yes, Joshua." She squirmed the tiniest bit, as though trying to find a comfortable position. It might be difficult for her because she was sitting right on his cock, and it was harder and thicker than he could ever remember it being.

"How can I trust you?" This was all part of the game he loved so much. Here he could let go and play out the darker of his impulses—to control, to take, to possess. See. Want. Have.

"You'll have to check," she replied. "Though shouldn't we go inside?"

He reached out and picked up his cell with his free hand, pushing one number and connecting to the security room. He put them on speaker. She needed to understand what she was up against in order for the game to be fair. "Landon?"

"This is Burke," the deep voice replied. "Shane's on patrol. What can I do for you?"

"Burke, I would like to fuck my submissive on the third-floor balcony. Is anyone watching us? Can you see any cameras pointed our way?"

A low, masculine chuckle came across the line. "No, Mr. Hunt. And given the angle relative to the beach, you should enjoy your evening without worry. The only peepers I would worry about would be your next door neighbor, and Jared is out for the night."

"I wouldn't care if he wasn't. Keep up the good work." He hung up and his hand tightened. "I would prefer when we're playing that you don't question me like that. I know where I want to fuck you. I know when I want to fuck you, and I'm in charge. If I want you in the middle of a crowded freeway, your only response is a yes or a no. Not to question me."

She seemed to relax back against him, as though she was giving up the struggle and choosing to submit. "Yes, Joshua. Yes, I understand, and yes to the sex. Please."

He liked the breathy little *please* and loved how she squirmed. Still, he wasn't absolutely sure she'd obeyed him, and he was a man who required proof. He slid his hand up her thigh. "Spread your legs for me."

Siren Enslaved
Texas Sirens Book 3
By Lexi Blake writing as Sophie Oak
Coming Spring 2018

Julian Lodge has everything a man could want. He's rich, successful and owns the most exclusive BDSM club in Dallas. But something is missing.

Finn Taylor has worked his way up in the world from humble beginnings in Willow Fork, Texas. The only thing he still loves in his hometown is Danielle Bay. He never told her he was actually bisexual, and he never confessed his love for her. Now she's getting married, and Finn is sure he's lost his chance with the only person he'll ever love.

Julian's vacation to the Barnes-Fleetwood ranch brings them all together. After Dani jumps into Julian's car while fleeing her wedding, Julian knows he has to have her. But nothing is easy in Willow Fork. A danger from Julian's past threatens them all. Julian will have to convince both Dani and Finn that being his will be the best decision they ever made.

About Lexi Blake

Lexi Blake lives in North Texas with her husband, three kids, and the laziest rescue dog in the world. She began writing at a young age, concentrating on plays and journalism. It wasn't until she started writing romance that she found success. She likes to find humor in the strangest places. Lexi believes in happy endings no matter how odd the couple, threesome or foursome may seem. She also writes contemporary Western ménage as Sophie Oak.

Connect with Lexi online:

Facebook: Lexi Blake
Twitter: authorlexiblake
Website: www.LexiBlake.net

Sign up for Lexi's free newsletter here.

94878577R00076

Made in the USA
Columbia, SC
01 May 2018